This marriage
end.

Wendy was merel
dinners and the mothe of his children.

He'd never considered how his scheme would affect a flesh and blood woman, a woman he was beginning to know as both caring and vulnerable.

Josh shoved a hand through his hair. His one great love had always been his work. That's where he used up his passions every day. Oh, he knew how to seduce a woman and he knew how to please, but to show love? *That*, he didn't know how to do.

A hard fist of disgust twisted his gut. *No!* He would not indulge himself sexually before the marriage simply to satisfy baser needs. Maybe he was a business shark, but he wasn't completely without scruples.

"Okay, smart guy," he grumbled, "how do you plan to keep her in her clothes for the next two months?" Here was yet another experience he was totally unfamiliar with—the *preservation* of a woman's virtue.

Dear Reader

In Mills & Boon Enchanted® we delight in bringing you the ultimate in single men, from bachelor bosses to heart-melting millionaires, desert sheikhs to desperate daddies, in our mini-series ***Bachelor Territory***.

Tough but tender? You bet! Strong but silent? Well, not any more. These great romances all feature the hero's point of view.

This month's book is BOARDROOM BRIDEGROOM by Renee Roszel, where tycoon Joshua Raven has to marry to bring about a business merger. He has to win Wendy's affections—and fast! Little does he expect her to have her own agenda—she'll not stay in the marriage for anything less than love!

Happy reading!

The Editors

Some men have everything–except the right woman!

BOARDROOM BRIDEGROOM

BY

RENEE ROSZEL

To Lenore Roszel, Eva Parrack and Anna May Bancroft—
three women I love, but don't tell often enough

All the characters in this book have no existence outside the imagination of the author, and have no relation whatsoever to anyone bearing the same name or names. They are not even distantly inspired by any individual known or unknown to the author, and all the incidents are pure invention.

First published in Great Britain 1998
Harlequin Mills & Boon Limited,
Eton House, 18-24 Paradise Road, Richmond, Surrey TW9 1SR

ISBN 0 263 81461 0

Set in Times Roman 10½ on 12 pt.
02-9902-49774 C1

Printed and bound in Norway
by AIT Trondheim AS, Trondheim

CHAPTER ONE

JOSHUA RAVEN rested an elbow on the antique mantel, half listening to the gushy blonde socialite, who was spilling out of her gown. Tonight he couldn't be bothered with simpering coquettes. Tonight was the beginning of the end of his quest to own Maxim Enterprises. All he had to do was marry Gower Isaac's daughter. What was her name again? Mindy, Sandy? No. Wendy. That was it. He must not forget.

Smiling at appropriate moments in the blonde's conversation, he scanned the elegant living room. Decorated in shades of peach and rust reds, the Georgian-style salon seemed to be eternally bathed in sunset.

Josh's scowling host, Gower Isaac, met his gaze and shrugged. Clearly the head of Maxim Enterprises was as distressed by his daughter's tardiness as Josh.

With another noncommittal murmur toward the buxom socialite still babbling at his elbow, he glanced at his watch. Almost half-past eight. Gower's daughter was over an hour late, and Josh was growing bored.

Ordinarily he would make a brief appearance at inane corporate functions like this, then leave with an excuse about "pressing business matters." But tonight was different. Tonight, he was being presented to the Maxim Enterprises's executives as their next CEO. The only remaining element, vital to the deal, was the tardy Miss Wendy Isaac. She didn't know it, but she was about to meet her future husband—*if* she ever arrived.

A bit "odd" Gower had called his only child. *Odd.*

Josh closed his eyes in a grimace of resignation. Loveless marriages were sometimes necessary in negotiating multimillion-dollar deals. He only hoped the Odd-Miss-Isaac would arrive soon. He wanted to get on with the chore of wooing her.

Gower had grimly presented the stipulation of Josh's marriage to his daughter, obviously believing it would be a hard condition to swallow. But Josh was a pragmatist. He knew the ways of the world. People married for many reasons, only one of which was love.

For years, gaining control of Maxim Enterprises had been his dream. Nothing was going to stand in his way. *Nothing.* Especially not one odd-little-duck of a woman—who apparently had the notion she must be adored by the man she married.

He heard a loud cough and his gaze shot to Gower. The older man headed toward the room's double-doored entrance where a woman stood. In jeans and a voluminous sweatshirt, she looked laughably out of place among the tuxedos and spangled gowns. The woman waved at Gower and took a step backward, as though just checking in to let him know she was either coming or going. It didn't appear that she had any intention of joining the gathering.

Josh watched as Gower Isaac took the woman's arm, thwarting her escape. His ruddy face grew redder, and though his comments were whispered, it was clear the rotund little man was agitated. The woman smiled, and gave him a hug. If this was the tardy, Odd-Miss-Wendy-Isaac, Josh had to give her points for not being intimidated by her scowling father. She and Josh seemed to be the only two people at the cocktail party who weren't cowed by the little dictator.

His glance shifted from Isaac to scan the woman's

face. She wasn't a beauty. Her features lacked the fleshy lushness current high fashion considered elegant. Her hair was muddy brown, straight and pulled back in a ponytail. Displaced strands danced about her face. Yet, when she smiled at her father, Josh decided she had a nice mouth. The friendly expression lit up her face, and his lips quirked in response. She might be odd, tardy and woefully underdressed, but she had an infectious grin.

He was surprised when she turned to look at him. Her smile faded slightly, and she squinted as though in concentration as her father spoke, his manner unmistakably agitated. With a quick glance back at the bald man, she tweaked his thin nose and began to wend her way toward Josh.

He noticed she had on jogging shoes, and recalled the slogan for that brand. *Go for it!* He had a feeling not only the shoes, but Wendy Isaac herself, lived by that philosophy.

As she advanced on him like a general leading troops, he wondered what her father had said. *Wendy, dear, this man is helping me avoid a hostile takeover by purchasing Maxim Enterprises as my White Knight. To keep control of the company in the family, I'm forcing him to marry you. Now go make nice.*

Josh didn't believe Gower said anything like that. The older man had warned him that Wendy had vowed she didn't intend to be a pawn in any business deal the way her mother had been. She would marry for love or not at all. Besides, as the young woman marched his way, she was smiling. He didn't think her expression would be particularly amicable if her father had told her the truth.

Josh found himself turning to face her as she came up

to him. The poor blonde at his side stopped chattering, apparently realizing she was being openly ignored.

Wendy thrust out a hand. "Hello, Mr. Raven." When he grasped her fingers, she shook his hand. Actually shook it—quaintly unsophisticated for a woman of her breeding. "Dad tells me we should meet. I'm sorry I don't have time to chat. I just dropped by to pick up some stuff. I'm on my way out."

Josh watched her animated face, noting her eyes were bigger than he'd first thought. They were an unusual shade of blue, more like neon purple. Pretty eyes, actually, and they smiled at him with a guileless quality he hadn't expected from the offspring of a cunning tyrant like Gower Isaac.

"I teach adult literacy classes on Tuesday, Thursday and Saturday night," she was saying. "Dad always forgets. I'm sorry I have to run, but the man I'm tutoring—well, he's forty and he was so ashamed when he started class—I mean having lied all his life about not being able to read. But he's trying hard. I wouldn't cancel on him for the world. Dad's horribly angry with me."

She shrugged as though accustomed to being a disappointment to her father, but her grin exhibited an undaunted quality he found commendable. "Dad tells me you're the White Knight who rode in to save Maxim from those raiders. That's wonderful. I do hope we'll have a chance to chat sometime." She flicked up her wrist to check her watch. "Wow, eight-thirty. I really must go."

She dropped his hand, gave him one more genuinely friendly second of eye-to-eye contact, and spun away on those go-for-it shoes. An instant later she was gone.

"Nice to meet you, too, Wendy," he murmured with a wry chuckle. Mentally he surveyed his ego. Just the tiniest puncture wound. He would heal. But it was clear that Odd-Little-Wendy-Isaac didn't find Joshua Raven as irresistible as the tabloids continuously suggested. He had a feeling this purple-eyed dynamo might not be the easy conquest he'd expected her to be. He'd have to lay it on thick.

"I'm embarrassed, my boy." Josh felt a heavy paw on his shoulder. "Damned girl has a mind of her own."

Josh turned to see Gower, his face a wrinkled portrait of aggravation. Still experiencing ironic amusement at being brushed off so thoroughly, he grinned at the older man. "You warned me she was odd, Gower. To be honest, I thought she was refreshing."

Gower's frown didn't ease. "You're a gentleman, my boy." He brightened. "Say, what if I invite you to dinner tomorrow?"

Josh slipped his hands into his tux pants' pockets. "Does your daughter teach anybody to do anything on Sunday nights?"

Gower grunted in disgust. "I don't think so." He shook his head. "No, I remember a charity open house last month. She went with me, but it was like pulling teeth. That was on a Sunday night."

Josh forced himself to hold on to his smile. The man was an arrogant son of a gun. The only downside to their alliance, besides the demand that Josh marry his daughter, was Gower's other deal-breaker requirement—that the older man be installed on Josh's board of directors. Since Josh had no choice if he was to realize his dream, he had acquiesced. Ironically, agreeing to the concession that Gower Isaac be underfoot had been harder to accept than the prospect of marrying a woman he'd never met.

"I'll make sure she's home—even if I have to tie her to a chair," Gower vowed, teeth gritted.

Josh's brows dipped for an instant, before he restored his grin. "Fine."

"Then you can start your seduction."

Josh felt an unpleasant twinge. As Gower glanced away to wave at someone across the room, he stared at the shorter man. How could any father talk about his own flesh and blood like she was a brood mare, to be sold to the highest bidder? Unfortunately, he could hardly cast stones. After all, he was the *buyer* in this bargain, and Wendy Isaac was just another piece of merchandise exchanging hands. When Gower turned back, he patted Josh on the shoulder. "All right, my boy, we'll see you tomorrow night. Six-thirty."

Nodding, he shoved all thoughts from his mind except his ultimate goal. Maxim Enterprises—the plum of plums—when combined with his own company, would make him one of the wealthiest men in America.

To that end, wide-eyed Wendy Isaac would soon be swept off her feet by an adoring Joshua Raven—at least that's what she would believe.

Wendy liked the butler's quarters on her father's estate. Cluttered with books and smelling of pipe tobacco, it was cozy and welcoming, just like the man who resided there. She'd known Millville all her life. He was like a grandfather to her. She missed him and his dog, Agnes, more than she missed her father—a sad commentary on her family.

She squatted on the woven rug to pet the old Irish setter. "How are you doing, Aggie, girl?"

The dog lifted her head and licked Wendy's hand. "We've missed you, too. That's why I brought Al to see you." She stroked her albino crow on the head. The bird was perched atop a magazine stand, beside the coffee table. Wendy glanced at her pet. "What do you say, Al? Aren't you happy to see Aggie?"

The crow was pure white, from the tip of her beak to her snowy claws. The only color she could boast was the light pink of her eyes. Lifting a foot as though in a wave, the bird squawked, "Al loves Aggie. Al loves Aggie."

Wendy laughed. "Yes, and Aggie loves—"

"What do you think you're doing, *girl?*"

Accustomed to her father's growling, Wendy hardly flinched. But Agnes crawled beneath the coffee table with a whimper. Al flapped from her perch with a high-pitched screech, a second later thudding down hard on Wendy's head. In panic, the crow's claws scraped at her scalp, not quite breaking the skin. *"Ouch!"* Wendy yelped, thanking heaven she'd just clipped Al's claws.

She fumbled to stand, grimacing at her father. "Dad! Look what you've done! You've scared Al." She tried to pry her crow's talons from the curls she'd painstakingly created with her curling iron, but the bird pecked at her fingers. "*Ouch.* Drat." The three-pound bird an unwieldy crown, Wendy narrowly eyed her father. "You really have a way with animals."

She watched his steely eyes scan her where the crow held her hair in a death grip. With his most imposing scowl, his gaze trailed down her body to her feet. He was making it painfully clear he didn't think her green, cotton sundress and sandals were appropriate for tonight's dinner party.

"Is that what you're wearing?"

She shook her head at his attitude, then winced as the move caused Al to clutch tighter. "Dad, why do you want me at this dinner? I'm sure you and Mr. Raven have business to discuss. Usually you tell me my chattering gives you a headache.''

''I thought you and Josh should get to know each other, that's all.'' He indicated her with a wave. ''Did you leave any clothes here after you moved out? Surely there's something you could change into.''

Trying to hold her temper, she moved up to him and patted his cheek. ''This isn't nineteen fifty-five when women wore girdles and white gloves. Mr. Raven is buying the *business,* not me. I'm sure he won't care what I'm wearing.''

Her father crossed his arms over his ample paunch. Dressed in a navy silk suit, he looked impeccable. ''Dammit girl, take that ridiculous bird off your head. I don't want him to think you're insane.'' The melodious sound of a doorbell intruded, and a look that seemed almost fearful crossed Gower's features. ''There he is, now.''

Wendy was confused by his nervous demeanor. Her father never got rattled. She watched, concerned, as he glanced through the door into the kitchen. ''There goes Millville.'' When he faced her again, he grimaced. ''Do something about that damned bird!''

''Shhhh!'' she admonished as Al let out a screech and clutched tighter. ''Shouting only makes it worse. Unless you want me to cut a big bald spot on the top of my head, she'll be there until she calms down.'' Wendy took her father's hand. ''You know when Al's upset she can't be forced to do anything. If you're very quiet for fifteen or twenty minutes, I can probably coax her down.''

He moved with her most of the way through the kitchen, then halted, dragging her to a stop. She noticed the staff had frozen in an amusing tableau, clearly unaccustomed to seeing albino crows attached to women.

"You don't mean to tell me you're going to meet Mr. Raven with that—that thing on your head?"

She smiled impishly. The only time he really paid attention to her was when he was outraged at her. It felt good to be noticed. "Why shouldn't Mr. Raven meet Al? With a name like his, they already have a lot in common. They'll want to chat."

"Wendy!" Gower shouted, but when the bird scolded, he ran a beefy hand over his face. "Where did I go wrong?" he muttered. "You're not a child any longer. You're a twenty-five-year-old woman. Women don't greet guests with wild fowl in their hair!"

She felt a tinge of pity. Pathologically correct and infinitely self-centered, the poor man would never understand how much of his distress he brought on himself. She reached out to hug him but he brushed away her hands. "Don't do that! You know how I hate gush."

She sighed, struggling to remain positive, but refusing to be cowed. "Just remember whose fault it is that Al is in my hair, Dad." Wendy took his arm. "Besides, haven't you already apologized to Mr. Raven about me—being eccentric? I thought that was the first thing you told people."

His frown was grim and vaguely sheepish.

"See!" She was only slightly insulted that her father felt it necessary to apologize for her, accustomed to it by now. "You've brilliantly prepared him, already."

"Nevertheless, I *forbid* you to see Mr. Raven with that monstrosity on your head!"

"You forbid me?" Wendy might not be much like her father in most ways, but she *was* his daughter. And like her father, she did not allow herself to be dictated to. She met his disapproving eyes without flinching.

"You're mistaking me for my mother," she said quietly. Taking his elbow, she tugged. "Come on."

Though Gower was stiff as a board, she coaxed him toward the front door. If she were totally honest, she didn't relish meeting Mr. Raven with a crow in her hair any more than she relished sitting through a stuffy business dinner. Deciding she might as well give them both a break, she offered, "On the other hand, I could sneak out the back and go home."

"No, I—" he began roughly, then seemed to think better of his tone. "I want you to join us this evening." He glanced at her as they headed down the hall to the foyer, his gray eyes narrowed on the crow. "Why did you bring that bird over here, anyway?"

"Al was depressed. I've been gone a lot. I figured she'd enjoy seeing old Agnes and Millville."

His expression dubious, he growled, "Depressed? How can a bird be depressed?"

"Al was barking. She always barks when she misses Agnes."

Gower shook his head, looking befuddled, and Wendy could hardly keep from laughing. Feeling concern for anybody or anything that didn't affect *his* bottom line was an utterly foreign concept for her father.

She tried to love her father, crusty old bully that he was. After all, he was the only family she had. He'd made her mother's life miserable, but sadly her mother hadn't had any backbone. Wendy had learned how *not* to handle her dad by watching her mom continually knuckle under to his demands. She'd tried many tactics over the years, and finally found it best to simply ignore his tantrums, be as kind and attentive as she could, but refuse to lose herself in the force of his intimidating presence.

Her attitude of affectionate insubordination drove him batty. She didn't mean for it to, but that seemed to be the only way to handle him. She refused to be swallowed up by the man—by his selfish demands—the way her poor mother had been. So she became an individual to be reckoned with, on her own terms.

As they entered the foyer, their heels tapped out a staccato rhythm on the marble floor, the domed ceiling echoing their steps. The oval room, complete with a majestic, winding staircase, was white on white, from the classical columns to the Georgian moldings and cornices that embellished the place. Wendy thought wryly that in all this fancy white decoration, Mr. Raven might not notice Al cleaving to her head.

When Millville, their aging butler, stepped back from the double doors to allow their guest entry, Wendy couldn't help but take singular notice. Dressed in black, Joshua Raven was a sharp contrast to the surroundings. Though his attire was casual, trousers and a polo shirt, he was every inch as striking today as he had been in his tuxedo.

She vividly recalled her first sight of him. Standing there, tall and elegant across the room, his black eyes trained on her. She'd felt an electrical shock when their glances met, as though she'd been in the crosshairs of a rifle. She'd shaken off the irrational thought, but she hadn't forgotten how it made her feel. She supposed any man who clawed his way up from poverty to reach such extraordinary success at his age, probably looked at everybody as potential prey.

She watched as his gaze fell on her—and her crow. Those ebony eyes widened a fraction. She sensed the tiny reaction was quite a show of emotion for a man accustomed to keeping his own counsel. Waving broadly, she urged her balky father forward. ''Hello, Mr. Raven. Welcome.''

Their guest seemed to have difficulty pulling his glance from her headgear. When their eyes met, she smiled. ''If you're wondering, this is Al.'' She reached up and stroked the bird along its wing and was promptly pecked for her trouble. ''Ouch!''

''Miss?'' Millville asked in his sedate way. ''Shall I take her?''

''Millville, I'd love it, but Daddy *shouted.*'' She shrugged.

The butler nodded in understanding. ''I'll fetch the persuader.''

''Oh, what a wonderful idea,'' Wendy said. ''I'd forgotten about that.''

''What is it?'' Josh asked, his lips curling. ''A slingshot?''

Wendy laughed. ''No. Al likes Twinkies. Sometimes it works.''

''Ah.'' Josh's perusal lingered on the crow for another moment before he peered at Gower. Wendy noticed her father's face was a shade of red she'd never seen before. ''Dad would rather I didn't wear Al to dinner,'' she teased. ''Actually, I think he'd like to *have* Al for dinner.''

Josh Raven's husky laugh echoed in the cavernous room. ''Eat crow? Gower Isaac? I know people who'd pay big money to see that.''

Startled by his wit, she giggled. Reaching up, she stroked Al's soft feathers and was relieved when the bird didn't peck at her. ''I like Mr. Raven, Al. What's your opinion?''

''You're a pretty boy,'' the bird blurted. ''Kiss me, pretty boy.''

"Oh, lord," Gower muttered.

Josh laughed, and once again the room rumbled pleasantly with his mirth. "A white crow that talks and doubles as a hat. I'm impressed." His glance shifted to Wendy. "By the way, please call me Josh."

"Thank you—Josh." Wendy found their guest to be unlike anything she'd expected. Oh, she'd known he was handsome, even before last night. Anybody who'd lingered in the checkout line in a supermarket knew his face. He was quite the lady's man, according to the tabloids—naturally, she only *scanned* the stories. Cameras loved him, making him look darkly seductive in every grainy photo she'd seen.

As she examined his face, she had to rethink that notion. Cameras didn't do justice to that cleft chin or the shadowed hollows beneath his strong cheekbones. And those deep-set eyes. Sparkling with vitality, they were surrounded by lashes so thick and long they looked artificial. It was widely known that Joshua Raven had been born with a double set of eyelashes—a rare birth defect any woman in her right mind would commit murder for.

"Kiss me, pretty boy!" Al repeated, drawing Wendy out of her musings.

"I'm not into feathers, Al, old buddy," Josh said with a crooked grin. "But thanks anyway."

Deciding he'd passed a test she hadn't been aware she was giving, she reached up and stroked the crow's soft breast. "Okay, Al, you've made your point." She met those darkly sexy eyes. "Al's short for Alberta. She's a shameless flirt. We think her former owner was a lady of the evening."

"Alberta has clearly made a change for the better."

She experienced a flutter of admiration. No wonder he was so popular with women. If he could make her feel as though having a crow on her head was perfectly proper dinner attire—even as it shrieked off-color propositions at him—then he deserved his reputation as a charmer.

The sound of footfalls attracted their attention. "Oh, good, the cavalry's coming." She turned to see Millville approach. Looking starched and professional in his dark uniform, he carried a shaft of sponge cake. "Come to Uncle Millie, Alberta," he cooed. "You and I and Agnes shall have a Twinkies pig-out in my quarters."

With a squawk, Al fluttered off Wendy's head, pulling out reluctant strands of hair in the process. Landing on Millville's outstretched arm, the crow tore into the cake.

"Thanks, Millville." She ran her fingers through her ruined curls in an attempt to minimize the damage. "I'll pick her up before I go."

"No hurry, miss," the old man offered. "Agnes and I have missed this naughty girl."

"Millville," Gower said in an unusually restrained tone. "Get rid of that refugee from a corn field, and tell Cook our guest would like to eat."

As Millville exited the foyer, Al squawked, "Pretty boy—*kiss* me!" spraying Twinkies crumbs into the air. The crow's high-pitched plea snapped Wendy from an odd trance, and it struck her that she'd been staring at Josh with an inane grin on her face.

Though she was positive he was accustomed to women gaping longingly at him, she hadn't thought of herself as the type of ninny to be drawn in by a playboy's charisma. Chagrin heated her cheeks. *How superficial!* Turning toward her father, she forced an offhand tone. "I'm starving, Dad. Let's eat."

She was starting to have major regrets about meeting this man with a crow on her head. But it was too late to alter his impression. The best course was to get this dinner over as quickly as possible and hope that Joshua Raven would be charitable and forget he ever met her.

The multitiered stone patio was one of Wendy's favorite spots, and one of the very few things about her mother's ancestral home she missed. Located in Kennilworth, a suburb on the North Shore of Chicago, Wendy had grown up in one of the most affluent communities in the country. Hers had been a beautiful if cheerless home. Fighting a bout of melancholy at the memories, she gazed out over the calm waters of Lake Michigan. Sunset-tinged sailboats skimmed along its glassy surface. The lake was so vast, it looked like an ocean, flowing out beyond the horizon as far as the eye could see.

The cool breeze off the lake grew nippy as the sun sank low in the evening sky. She shivered, rubbing her arms.

"Are you cold?"

She faced Josh. Her father had excused himself sometime ago, saying he'd forgotten an appointment. So here she was, left to entertain Joshua Raven. *Alone.* Gower Isaac rarely left her to entertain his business associates. But she blessed him for choosing this time, and this man.

Josh was smiling at her as though he thought she was quite wonderful to behold. She couldn't help but smile back. The setting sun did eerie things to his dark hair, making it gleam with subtle fire.

Meeting his gaze, she had the strangest sensation. His eyes glittered with a light that was almost predatory. The thought flashed through her mind that a raven was sometimes thought of as a bird of ill omen. *How silly.* Anything ominous she'd imagined in his glance had to be a caprice of the sunset. Josh Raven was their White

Knight, for heaven's sake. Certainly not an enemy. She mentally shook herself, trying to hold on to the subject at hand. "It—it gets chilly very quickly when the breeze is off the lake."

"Let me get you a sweater." He rose to his feet.

Just then Millville came outside to clear away the dessert plates and bring more coffee. The darling man had a shawl draped over his arm. She accepted it gratefully. "You read minds, Millie?"

He nodded, loading the remainder of the dishes on a tray. "More coffee, miss?"

"No, I'm fine."

Millville shifted to look at Josh. "Sir?"

Josh shook his head.

"Then, I'll leave you two to enjoy the evening," the butler murmured before silently disappearing into the house.

Wendy was adjusting the shawl when she felt a hand on her shoulder. "Let me."

She glanced up to see Josh smiling down at her. With a nod, she released the white crocheted fabric. After he placed the shawl about her, he skimmed a finger along her shoulder. The brief touch was astoundingly sensual, sending a ripple of excitement through her. "There." He moved to her side and held out a hand. "Why don't we walk down to the water? I love the lake."

Her brain went foggy as she watched herself accept his hand. This was not how she'd expected the evening to go at all. She'd anticipated sitting in the big, impersonal dining room playing hostess with a plastered-on smile, keeping her mouth shut per her father's usual orders.

Gower Isaac had made it no secret that he'd been immensely displeased that his only child was a girl, and worse, one who preferred volunteer work to making money. He usually allowed her to forgo hostess duties, grousing that he never knew what she might say to embarrass him—from cajoling business associates into investing in Project Literacy or the Society for the Prevention of Cruelty to Animals, to brazenly counseling them to quit smoking.

After disappointing her father last night she'd decided not to turn him down, and had consented to be his hostess. However, because of her past experiences with strained dinner parties, she had dreaded tonight.

For once in her life, the experience was delightful. Her father had hardly spoken, allowing the conversation to flow, with business barely intruding at all. Josh proved to be a fascinating conversationalist. Wendy had been enthralled and the meal she'd expected to drag, simply flew. Then, as dessert was about to be served, Gower Isaac abruptly withdrew.

She didn't understand it, but she wasn't looking a gift horse in the mouth. She liked Josh Raven. She liked him as a person, something she hadn't expected to do. And his drop-dead good looks didn't hurt. Every time he grinned, her pulse went into a jig as mad and thrilling as the footwork in the musical extravaganza "Riverdance."

"You have a lovely home, Wendy," he said, drawing her back.

They ambled along a stone path winding through the lavish gardens toward a retaining wall, where a stone stairway led down to the lake.

She clasped her hands before her as they walked. "It is nice. But I don't live here."

She could feel his eyes on her. "Really? Why not?"

She smiled, but didn't glance his way. "If Gower Isaac were your father, would you?"

His low laughter was mellow.

"It's not that I don't love him," she said, feeling the need to explain.

"You don't have to tell me." His pause drew her gaze. "Just between us, I wouldn't want to live with your father, either."

"But it's not that you don't *love* him," she quipped.

His lips quirked. "I love him like the father I never wanted."

She burst out laughing, elated by their mutual opinion of her father, and even more, the fact that he wasn't afraid to say so. "I can tell you didn't let Daddy browbeat you in this deal," she said. "For once old Growling Gower met a man he couldn't make dance to his tune. You should be proud."

Some rueful emotion skittered across his features. Or did it? The light was fading and she couldn't be sure. The breeze picked up, ruffling her hair. She pulled the shawl closer about her, but it was too thin to do much good.

"Maybe this will help." Josh draped an arm about her, drawing her close.

She was amazed by her melting reaction. But then, Josh Raven wasn't one of those pathetic conformists she usually dated, who were more interested in currying favor with her father than in being with her. Josh was a successful, tough-minded man who had galloped in on his white charger and saved her father's company.

Now it was her father who was nervous in *Josh's* presence. That realization made her smile. Instead of stiffening and drawing away, she found herself nestling into the crook of his arm. His aftershave wafted about her, a sultry scent of summer nights and cedar. She inhaled deeply, enjoying the aroma.

What's going on, here? her brain cried. Something rosy-pink was clouding her mind. Why did she feel she'd known Joshua Raven all her life? What was it about his touch, his nearness, that made her want to know him—very, very well—for the rest of her days?

"Is that better?" His warm breath stirred the hair at her temple.

She glanced up, struck again by the staggering beauty of those eyes. Her voice deserted her, and all she could do was nod.

"Good." He grinned, a crooked slash of straight, white teeth.

He shifted to gaze out at the lake, growing indistinguishable from the sky in the dimness. As they strolled, he continued to hug her to him. The only sound in the growing dusk was the pleasant lapping of water on sand, and the distant buzzing of a motorboat far out on the water.

They reached the end of the lawn and Josh turned to face her, propping a hip against the stone rail of the retaining wall that separated them from the beach ten feet below. "Would you like to walk on the sand?"

She hadn't done that in years. "I think I would."

He took her arm and helped her down the steep staircase. At the bottom step she sat down and tugged off her sandals. He pulled off his loafers and socks, then rolled up his trouser legs. With a sidelong glance, he said, "If it were warmer, we could swim."

She laughed. It had been eighty-nine degrees that afternoon. Warm for the first day of June. But the lake would be too cold for swimming for at least a month.

She indicated her dress. "I couldn't swim in this."

"You're right." His grin was sexy. "The dress would definitely have to come off."

As his gaze held hers, a rush of heat invaded her body. Oh, gracious! What was wrong with her? Why wasn't she slapping his face? Why did she have a scary feeling that if it were July, she'd be tearing off her clothes? "What a shame it isn't warmer," she finally managed, hoping she was kidding.

"Damn shame." He took her hand and pulled her up to stand.

As they strolled along, she couldn't help but ask, "Do you skinny-dip a lot?"

"Never have."

She peered at him. "Oh, *please.*"

"No. Really."

She smirked, unconvinced. Some unruly imp inside her took the conversational reins. "And you've never made love, I suppose." She was surprised at herself. She didn't talk like this to a man she'd hardly met. Actually she didn't talk like this at all!

"Never made love?" His eyes twinkled. "Let me think."

She grinned, warming to the flirting game, unfamiliar though it was. "I bet you've never even kissed a woman."

"How did you guess?"

"We are now entering the Twilight Zone, folks," she said with a laugh.

His irresistible grin did insidious things to her insides. Needing a break from the lure of those eyes, she forced her gaze away.

He tugged on her hand and she realized he'd come to a halt. When she turned, his expression had lost all humor. "What?" she asked, strangely breathless, wondering at his mood change.

He inclined his head, the gesture unmistakable. He was telling her to come to him, though he was only a step away. "What do you want?" Her heart tripped over itself with womanly knowledge. She knew. And she was shocked to discover she wanted it, too.

He reached out, cupping her nape with gentle fingers. His thumb caressed the underside of her jaw, the sensation wildly erotic. She grew weak—and utterly willing—as he drew her face to his.

CHAPTER TWO

JOSH sat at his massive desk in his massive office, fighting off a massive headache. With a raw curse, he pushed up from his leather chair and stalked to stare out the window wall, overlooking Lake Michigan. Damn he felt like a worm, kissing the woman the way he had, leading her on.

But hadn't that been the point? Wasn't that the reason for the whole evening—to begin the ''Wooing of Wendy''? When he'd made his deal with Gower Isaac he simply hadn't realized what a lousy taste the underhanded sham would leave in his mouth.

Not her kiss, he realized. There had been nothing lousy about the taste of her kiss. The odd little woman who wore crows in her hair was certainly compatible enough in that area. And she wasn't all that odd-looking, either. In that green sundress, with her hair curling around her face, there was an innocent sexiness about her. Another bit of compatibility he hadn't expected from Isaac's lackluster description of his daughter. Of course Gower would have no inkling of anything like that about his Wendy. The old man saw her as his useless non-son. Well, useless except for manipulating her into unknowingly helping to keep company control in the family.

A stab of pity made him wince. Hell, he didn't want to pity the woman, he wanted to marry her. No. In truth, he wanted to get the marriage behind him so he could get on with running what would now be called Raven-Maxim Enterprises.

He was proud that his consumer software publishing company had grown to be one of the largest in the United States. Combined with Gower Maxim's holdings, consisting of newspapers, television and radio stations as well as several national magazines, Josh would have wealth and power beyond his wildest dreams. The debts Isaac had incurred over the past few years didn't bother Josh. All Maxim Enterprises needed was a revitalization. That would come with innovative business techniques, along with trimming corporate fat. The challenge excited him. He was in his element.

Only one thing put a damper on his enthusiasm—the obligatory wedding. Nevertheless, didn't he know that nothing truly valuable came without sacrifice? Didn't he learn from his struggle up from meager beginnings, with parents who'd married more from need than desire, that life was not a bouquet of thornless roses?

"A man has to do what a man has to do," he muttered, repeating the tired phrase he'd heard his father say more times than he cared to remember. "So get on with it, Raven," he ground out. Pivoting away from the million-dollar view, he returned to his huge chrome-and-glass desk and punched his intercom. "Miss Oaks, get me Miss Isaac."

After her brisk "Yes, sir," he started to release the button, then thought better of it. "No—send her a dozen roses with an invitation to dinner."

"Where shall I send them, sir?" his secretary asked.

He closed his eyes, weary irritation rushing through him. "I don't know. Call Gower's office. Somebody there can track her down."

There was a pause, then, ''Yes—sir. Should I say you'll be by to pick her up?''

He bit off a curse. ''Of course I'll pick her up. Make it eight o'clock and get me that address.''

''Yes, sir.'' Another pause. ''Did you want to look over the stock prospectus now, sir?''

''Hell—I forgot. Yes. *Now,*'' he barked, then realized what an ass he was being. This was totally unlike him. ''Miss Oaks,'' he added more gently. ''I'm sorry for snapping. It's been one of those days.''

''No problem, sir.'' She sounded relieved. ''We all have them.''

''Thanks, Miss Oaks.'' He managed to sound less aggravated than he felt. ''That will be all.''

Releasing the button he flung his hand through his hair, hoping the Odd-Miss-Isaac would be as pleasantly disposed toward a quick marriage as her crow apparently was to Twinkies. He wanted to get this wedding business over.

Pressing his knuckles against throbbing temples, he sagged back in his chair. ''Good lord, Raven, you've turned *yourself* into a blasted Twinkie!''

That evening, a few minutes before eight, Josh's chauffeur pulled to a stop in front of a brick apartment building in Evanston, a north Chicago suburb. Josh templed his hands before him, eyeing the place with diffidence. Though Evanston had its share of palatial lakefront homes, this apartment house was not in the most affluent section of town. Or even the middle class section. She certainly lived frugally, if her residence was any indication.

''Are you sure this is the right address, Mr. Raven?'' his chauffeur asked.

Josh tapped his pursed lips with templed index fingers, fighting an ironic grin. "I'm afraid so, Higgins."

"Would you like me to go get the lady for you, sir?"

Josh cleared his throat to hide a chuckle. Obviously Higgins wasn't aware that in his childhood, this modest, aging building would have seemed like a palace. No doubt his chauffeur thought Josh feared catching something from the great unwashed masses. "No, Higgins, I'll retrieve the lady myself."

"What if there's no elevator, sir?"

Josh worked at keeping his expression serious. "Let's not be negative, Higgins." He opened the door, stepping onto the sidewalk, then remembered something and tapped the chauffeur's window. When the young man lowered the glass Josh held out a hand. "Give me that sack."

Higgins's small features were already drawn down in a perplexed frown—an expression that became even more perplexed as he picked up the brown paper sack and handed it through the window.

"Thanks."

"Yes, sir." As the darkened window glass rose, Josh watched in amusement as his chauffeur shook his head, clearly dumbfounded.

When Josh turned away, he had to grin. He didn't think Higgins had ever been more confused than a few minutes ago when Josh asked him to pull into a nearby Quick-And-Go store and buy the box of Twinkies.

Dim yellow light from a street lamp illuminated a dandelion in his path, its yellow head poking through a crack in the walkway. Stepping around it, he followed an uneven cement walk to the front steps, eyeing the thin strip of yard in the gloom. The grass could use mowing.

He bounded up two cracked and chipped steps. Inside a peeling green door he found himself in a narrow hallway, the walls papered with green cabbage roses from some long bygone era. It didn't take more than a glance to determine that there was no elevator. Just four doors labeled 1A, B, C, and D.

Drawing a slip of paper from his suit coat, he confirmed his suspicion—5A. "Naturally."

He scowled at the staircase dividing 1A and B from C and D. The steps were steep and well-worn. "Miss Isaac-the-Odd," he muttered under his breath, "I salute your cardiovascular fitness."

With a determined set of his jaw, he started up the creaky stairs, reminding himself this was a small price to pay for the realization of his life's goal.

Wendy Isaac answered his knock with unsophisticated speed. The woman didn't seem to know the meaning of the term "feminine wiles," at least not the one about keeping a gentleman cooling his heels outside her door.

"Hello, Josh," she said with that contagious grin. Though a bit winded, he grinned back as he scanned her from head to toe. She wore a basic black dress that hugged her slim waist, giving her an appealing hourglass look. Her scent was light, like fresh air after a rain. He had a feeling it was soap rather than cologne. Nice, though, and refreshing, after some of the perfume-drenched debutantes he'd known.

Her brown hair was swept up in a casual pile, stray wisps framing her face. Though Josh knew such artful disarray was all the rage in woman's coiffures these days, he sensed that with Miss Isaac it was more due to her breezy lifestyle than a fashion statement.

She stepped away from the door to allow him entry, indicating a bouquet on an oval dining table. Though the piece of furniture was polished to a bright sheen, it looked as though it had come from a thrift shop. ''The roses are lovely Josh.'' Her cheeks grew pink. ''I'm so sorry about the lovely vase.'' She peered at him sheepishly. ''I'm afraid Alberta knocked my best one over and broke it. I had to borrow a mayonnaise jar from next door, and then I had to trim the stems to make them fit.'' She shook her head, looking pained. ''In Illinois, I think it's a felony to trim long-stemmed roses to fit into a mayonnaise jar.''

He found himself chuckling, his dour mood lifting somewhat. ''Only a misdemeanor, but we'll keep it just between us.'' He contemplated the small apartment, wondering why she lived like this. Surely she had a trust fund or an inheritance from her mother. The place was neat and clean, but everything had the look of second-hand stores and flea markets. As he surveyed the place, his glance once again fell on Wendy. She'd moved silently across the worn carpet to a green and brown plaid couch. Across one arm lay a black jacket that matched her sleeveless dress.

She picked it up and handed it to him.

As he helped her into it he heard a rustling sound. ''Kiss me, pretty boy!'' came the familiar challenge. Josh looked up in time to see a flurry of white feathers swoop in from another room.

The crow landed on the tabletop and gave the roses a piercing look. If Josh hadn't known better, he'd have thought the bird was finding fault with them. Suddenly he remembered the sack. ''Oh, I brought something for Alberta.''

Wendy looked at him, her expression one of surprise. ''Really?''

He held out the paper bag. ''You do the honors.''

Wendy took the sack and opened it, her astonished expression changing, softening into a lovely smile. ''Why, Josh...'' She shook her head as though in awe. ''That's so sweet.'' Lifting the box out, she wagged it at her crow. ''Look, you naughty girl. Josh brought you a present, too.''

Like a shot, Al was airborne, landing heavily on Wendy's outstretched sleeve. Ripping at the cardboard, Al squawked, ''Take it off, pretty boy! Take it all off!''

With a laugh, Wendy tossed the box to the couch and Al quickly fluttered after it. She faced Josh, those neon eyes shining. ''I think I'd better rescue all but one of those or she'll make herself sick.''

Intrigued by the bird's comical antics, Josh relaxed against the wall, crossing his arms before him. ''Who did you say owned Al before you did? The Happy Hooker?''

Though her back was to him, Josh watched her neck go red with embarrassment as she detached the box and its contents from Al's talons—all but one Twinkie, already mutilated beyond recognition. ''We're not sure who her first owner was. One day Millville found her perched on Daddy's patio table singing that song 'Bad to the Bone.' You know the one? Anyway, Millville loves animals so he tried lots of things to coax her to him.'' Wendy disappeared around a corner and Josh assumed she was putting the Twinkies away in a kitchen cabinet. When she returned, she smiled shyly. ''Anyway, what finally worked was a Twinkie.''

She shrugged. ''When Al's spicy vocabulary began to come out in dribs and drabs, we started having misgivings about her previous owner. We advertised in the lost and found section of the paper for a month, but nobody answered the ad.'' She stopped by the couch and lovingly stroked the crow's head. "Al's so smart and funny. I couldn't leave Daddy's house, and not bring her with me. I love her—vocabulary and all."

Josh glanced at the bird, perched on the sofa in the middle of shredded cellophane and Twinkies crumbs. Al eyed him back, her head cocked jauntily to one side, a glob of cream filling on her beak.

He grinned at the cocky little vixen. "What? No 'thank you,' young lady?"

Al inclined her head the other way, as though considering his request. Then with what looked like a wink of one pink eye, she squawked, "Cash. No checks!"

Josh felt a surge of absurd amusement and laughed. "You're welcome, you little hussy."

"Now, be good, Al," Wendy admonished. "If anybody tries to get in, you bark like Aggie and scare them away."

The crow flapped her wings threateningly and gave off a startling impression of a bloodthirsty Doberman. "Whoa." Josh grinned at Wendy. "Remind me never to cross that female."

As he smiled down at her, quiet seconds ticking by, Wendy lowered her gaze and fidgeted with her jacket as though straightening it. To Josh it looked more like a nervous gesture than a need to adjust her clothing. When she lifted her gaze to meet his once again, her cheeks were that bright peach color they seemed to be every time she made direct eye contact with him. "You don't have to worry about Al," she murmured. "She has a crush on you."

Placing his hand in the small of her back, he steered her out of the apartment. "How many men can say that about a crow they've just met?" he kidded.

Though he kept his grin in place, he thought cynically,

Good going, Josh, you've won the damn bird's affections, now you'd better get the woman's—and fast!

The restaurant on the ninety-fifth floor of the Hancock building served a variety of the best in international cuisine that Chicago had to offer. Unfortunately, Wendy couldn't taste a thing. Her whole body, tastebuds and all, were focused on the fact that she was actually out on a real live date with one of the most eligible bachelors in the country—and his attention was riveted to her every word.

He smiled all the time, laughing at her smallest funny story, appearing vitally interested in her passion for Project Literacy. How perfect could one evening be?

Perhaps another kiss? No, that would be too perfect. Nobody in the history of the world had ever experienced an evening *that* perfect. Under the cover of the table, she'd actually pinched herself several times to make sure she wasn't dreaming all this. She feared she'd have a good size bruise tomorrow.

Josh gazed into her eyes, smiling, his craggy features splendidly male in the candlelight. She found herself harking back to last night and the kiss they shared. His lips had been warm, masterful, yet beautifully sensitive. She'd learned a terrible and wonderful truth with that kiss.

It had been all too clear—a truth she hadn't wanted to form into a full-blown, rational thought. And that truth was, the instant Josh Raven smiled at her last night—with Al stuck to her head—she'd fallen hopelessly, irrevocably in love with him. She'd recognized that fateful moment somewhere on a subconscious level, but the protective part of her brain had tried desperately to keep it buried.

But Josh's kiss had released that truth from its captivity and she was forced to face it head-on. *She loved him.* What an awful thing to discover about a man who could get any woman he wanted—and according to the tabloids—*did.* When the roses and his dinner invitation came today, she'd almost died of both terror and joy. She didn't dare believe that he had been moved by their kiss, too. But she hadn't been strong enough to refuse his invitation.

In the companionable silence she ran her tongue along her upper lip as her thoughts drifted with warm, delicious memories of his kiss. Strains of something soft and classical served as a romantic backdrop while they sat there, communicating with their eyes. He sipped his coffee but his glance remained on her.

When he put his cup down, he smiled and she had to quell a tremor at the intimate beauty of it. She felt a prick of sadness, wishing she hadn't accepted for this evening. Being so near Josh Raven was cruel torture. This man could never think of her as anything but "the peculiar daughter of Gower Isaac," so why did she have to put herself through this? No doubt this evening was his way of ingratiating himself to "the family." She swallowed hard. It would have been kinder if he'd sent the Twinkies by courier and kept his distance.

"Wendy?" The sound of her name, spoken in a husky whisper, sent a delightful quiver skittering along her spine.

She nodded. "Hmmm?"

His big, warm hand slipped over hers and squeezed. "Let's get married."

She had been smiling at him. Dreamily indulging her schoolgirl fantasies. But with his touch and the softly spoken request, she blinked. Surely he'd said something completely ordinary, like "Pass the sugar," and her lovesick brain had garbled the request.

She picked up the china sugar bowl and lay it beside his coffee cup. His glance shifted with her movement to the bowl, then returned to her face. His brows dipped in what appeared to be puzzlement.

Wondering at her bizarre brain malfunction, she cast her gaze around the table. What could he have possibly asked for? There were only the salt and pepper shakers left to choose from, since he couldn't have asked her to pass him the candle. But did he really want salt or pepper on his black walnut cake? She stared at him, bewildered. "I'm sorry. I'm afraid I didn't hear you."

His expression eased into another charming smile. "There goes my ego. I ask a woman to marry me and she's not even paying attention." He squeezed her fingers. "Do I have your attention, now?"

She gaped. He'd said absolutely nothing about sugar, salt or pepper. He'd said something about *marriage.*

He leaned around the table and lightly kissed the shell of her ear. "Wendy." His breath caressed her cheek. "Say something." When he drew back so their glances could meet, his gaze was intense.

She felt her hand being squeezed again, and managed to shake herself out of the pleasant stupor the touch of his lips against her ear had induced. Her heart turned over with a mixture of excitement and mystification. He couldn't mean what it sounded like he meant, could he? Gorgeous men of the world didn't actually fall in love with blunt, headstrong oddballs like her. And they certainly didn't propose marriage on the first date. She was simply going to have to make a doctor's appointment to have her ears checked—or get herself committed—or both.

She shook her head, trying to clear whatever it was that was blocking her ears. "Forgive me, Josh, but—"

"I know this is sudden," he cut in. "But I have to tell you, Wendy. No other woman has made me feel this way before. I need you in my life."

She blinked, staring into his eyes. They were amazing eyes. And they seemed to have nothing more pressing to do than gaze lovingly in her direction. "Wendy?" Her name came quietly, this time with a hint of—of *what?* Desperation? Longing? Or possibly—dare she even think it—hurt?

"Yes, Josh?" High-pitched and feeble, her voice didn't sound like her at all.

His gaze never leaving her face, he lifted her hand and brushed a kiss across her knuckles. "Do you think you could care for me, Wendy?"

Her hand tingled from the stroke of his lips and lingering touch of his fingers. Her ear still sizzled from his kiss. Her body was hot all over, and she knew her face must be flaming, though she prayed the candlelight masked her blush. Flustered and timid, she lowered her glance to her neglected crème brûlée. "I—I..." Her throat closed and she couldn't squeeze any words past the lump that formed there.

"Wendy, Wendy," he whispered urgently, leaning nearer until their lips were hardly an inch apart. "I realize what I've said may frighten you away. Still, I can't help it. I'm a man of action. I don't know any other way than just to say what I feel."

She met his gaze, wide-eyed in her amazement. He couldn't actually be proposing marriage. She didn't have that kind of effect on men. Sure she'd had boyfriends, but never had she known any man who radiated such potency, was so ragingly sensual or so unabashedly male. And never in a million—no make that a trillion—years, would she have held out any foolish hope that such a man would look twice at her.

Let alone propose marriage!

He reached out with his other hand, curling gentle fingers about her nape, drawing her just close enough to lightly tease her lips with his. "I have frightened you." He drew away, but only far enough to speak.

She sucked in a shaky breath. "Yes," she admitted, pulling out of his touch. "This doesn't make sense. You can't possibly be in love with me. You've known me for little more than twenty-four hours."

He took her hand, refusing to let her pull away. "Haven't you heard, darling? It happens that way, sometimes."

She swallowed spasmodically. Yes, of course, she'd heard of love at first sight. She'd even experienced it—with Josh! But it couldn't have happened to him! He couldn't have fallen for her. This was a dream. She pinched herself again, and winced. No, she felt awake. Her pulse beat pounded so furiously in her brain, she feared for her skull. But this simply couldn't be real. He couldn't possibly mean it. "This is a very bad joke, Mr. Raven," she said, trying to sound stern.

His smile faded and he released her hand. Sitting back in his chair, he mouthed a curse and looked away. "I'm sorry, Wendy, I just—" His jaw bunched and flexed in agitation as he jerked out his wallet, retrieving a platinum charge card. "I was a fool to speak my mind. Of course, now I see my feelings are all one-sided. Forgive me for embarrassing you."

Though he was no longer touching her, her head still reeled and throbbed, her body trembled. She hesitated, staring, baffled. His eyes seemed to shimmer with sadness. What was going on here? Had what he'd proposed been honest? Had he meant it from the heart? She vacillated, floundering in conflicting emotions. There was nothing she wanted more than to spend the rest of her life at this man's side, bearing his children, being his loving wife.

He lifted a hand to signal the waiter who seemed to appear from nowhere to relieve him of his card. When the employee was gone, Josh faced her, his expression solemn. "Do you forgive me for my rashness?" He reached out as though intent on taking her fingers in his, but seemed to think better of it and lay his hand on the table. "I'm an impulsive fool."

His dark eyes exhibited a bleakness that was hard to witness and she had to suppress a scream of frustration at the back of her throat. *What had she done?* Had this been a real proposal—from a man she'd fallen so hopelessly in love with that she couldn't believe it when she heard it? Had she actually turned him down? Did this sort of crazy miracle happen to ordinary people like her?

He cleared his throat. "Well, what should we talk about?" he asked, sounding as though he was working at being nonchalant.

"Yes," she blurted. What good did it do to try and analyze the vagaries of falling in love? That was as fruitless and pointless as allowing this magnificent man to slip through her fingers. "I don't understand how it all happened so quickly, but *yes,* Josh. I'll marry you."

Reaching out, she lifted his hand from the tabletop, kissed his palm, then scanned his handsome face. "I didn't want to admit it even to myself..." she murmured through a tremulous sigh. "But when you kissed me last night, I knew, Josh. I knew I was in love with you."

His eyes, those marvelous, expressive dark eyes widened the smallest fraction, then narrowed slightly, and she wondered what flinty emotion flashed in their depths. Or was the rush of tears that blurred her vision responsible for the mysterious distortion?

''Darling,'' he said, his voice low. ''My darling, Wendy.''

She smiled through trembling lips. ''Oh—Josh.''

He took her face between his hands. They seemed so cool, so steady. ''You'll never know how happy this makes me.''

Her heart flew away, soared and dived in the heavens as tears of joy slid down her cheeks. ''How—how...'' Working at collecting her emotions she smoothed back a lock of his hair, loving the silk feel of it beneath her palm. She relished the thought of knowing this amazing man *much* more intimately—of loving him for the rest of her life as he so clearly loved her.

''Oh, Josh—'' Her voice breaking with happiness, she began again. ''Oh, Josh—darling—what have I done to deserve you?''

CHAPTER THREE

LIKE shooting fish in a barrel, Josh thought grudgingly. He was engaged, just like that. Exactly as he'd planned—to a woman he hardly knew. A woman who had professed to love him.

He walked out onto the balcony of his apartment, two floors above his suite of offices in one of Chicago's most prestigious high-rises. The view of Lake Michigan was beautiful, with city lights defining graceful undulations of the shoreline. Sometimes after a hectic day the view helped Josh relax. But not tonight. He'd returned his new fiancée to her apartment and left her there with one, chaste kiss. Closing his eyes, he slumped against the railing. "Well, Gower, it looks like you've bartered yourself a son-in-law."

The chiming of his doorbell brought his head up with a start. He glowered at his watch. "Midnight?" he muttered. "Who the hell could be dropping by at this hour?" He reentered a living room that reeked of classic richness and unhurried grace. At least that's what a recent article in *Architectural Monthly* had stated. He gave the room's low slung modern furnishings and distinctive artwork a disgruntled look. As far as he was concerned it looked like a pretentious interior designer's waiting room. He heard a sound and glanced toward the entryway in time to see his butler hurriedly donning a black suit coat. "I'll get it, Nelson." He waved off the portly man. "You go on to bed."

Nelson stifled a yawn and nodded his thanks, withdrawing silently to his quarters. Josh's shoes made a clipped rat-a-tat across the black granite foyer to the double-doored entry. One quick look through the peep-hole told him who was there. ''This is all I need,'' he grumbled under his breath. Opening the door, he manufactured a smile. ''Hello, Evelyn. You're looking well.''

The tall brunette swept past him, leaving a trail of designer fragrance in her wake. Once inside, she twirled around to face him. Her slim column dress of iridescent red organza was slit up one side to mid-thigh, showcasing a long, shapely leg.

Shiny, black hair swirled with her, falling into perfect order about her shoulders. Her smile was brilliant, expectant. ''You look like you're getting ready to go to bed.'' Her bright blue eyes narrowed speculatively as her glance slid over him. ''No tie, no jacket?''

He lifted a brow to indicate his doubt that she dropped in on many men at midnight to find them totally primed for an evening out. ''I don't know what came over me,'' he said, his tone purposely sardonic.

She gave Josh what he had come to think of as ''her best pout.'' ''I thought we might go dancing.'' She smiled slyly. ''Or—something.''

He closed the door and leaned against it, crossing his arms before him. ''You did, did you?'' He smiled at her, but didn't bother to keep the impatience from his voice. ''It's midnight, Evelyn. Tomorrow's a workday. Just because you can sleep until noon doesn't mean I can.''

She moved toward him and began to toy with his shirt collar. ''Don't be silly, Josh, dear. You're the boss. You can do anything you want.''

He gave her a level stare. ''Perhaps I want to get to work before noon.''

She skimmed a long fingernail over his lower lip. "What else do you want to do, sweets?" Her question was highly suggestive. Only a stone or a dead man could miss her meaning.

Here was another complication to his upcoming marriage. *The girlfriend.* His gut clenched, even though Evelyn Jannis wasn't technically his girlfriend. They'd merely gone out several times over the past few weeks. That was it. He'd made no promises and she'd asked for none. Nevertheless, Evelyn seemed to be broadly hinting she wanted to take their relationship to a higher level—or, more likely, she was feeling lusty. He reached up and took her wrist. "Evelyn, you're a lovely woman, and we've—"

"We certainly have," she cut in with a sultry laugh, lifting her free hand to run her fingers through his hair. "Come on, Josh, I'm not in the mood for chatting."

Pressing against him, she lifted her chin, giving him a "kiss me" look. He smiled without enthusiasm, firmly setting her away. "Listen to me, Evelyn." His sternness made her blink and stare.

"What?" she asked, her expression going wary. "What's so serious?"

He didn't think there was any point in beating around the bush. "I'm getting married."

She didn't move for a few seconds, then her lips parted in a stunned "Oh." "Married," she echoed, with barely any sound. Quickly, she seemed to gather her wits, and straightened her shoulders. "Who?" Her tone was hard, her pupils all but disappearing. "When did this happen?"

"Tonight. I'm marrying Gower Isaac's daughter."

She frowned for a second, then her face cleared. "Oh—it's *business.*" She smiled, looking relieved.

"You had me worried for a moment." Her arms came up to skim along his shoulders, then curl behind his neck, as she drew herself against him once more. "That needn't affect us, sweets. I'm a big girl. I know about these things."

He gritted his teeth. She was *definitely* feeling lusty! It was too bad the woman knew how to move her body to do the most damage to his resistance. Her nudging and rubbing was subtle, but ripe with erotic innuendo. "Josh," she prodded, lifting her lips toward his, "let's play."

He inhaled, the male animal in him battling with his promise of marriage to another woman. He may have set about this wedding scheme knowing he didn't love Wendy Isaac, but he had also set about it with honorable intentions—well, as honorable as the situation allowed.

He believed in the institution of marriage. His parents may have come together out of mutual need, but they'd come together with the belief that the vows they'd taken were sacred. Through poverty and hardship, they'd struggled together, trusted and depended on each other. Their union had been honest and upright.

Nostrils flaring with a determined inhale, he pulled her arms from about his neck. "I mean for this marriage to work, Evelyn. I won't be playing around."

Evidently not expecting to be set away for a second time, Evelyn stumbled a step, and Josh had to take her arm to steady her. She stared in visible disbelief. "Work?" She sounded incredulous. "What do you mean *work?* You aren't saying you love this woman, are you? I've never even heard you mention her. You haven't even said her name!"

"Wendy," he murmured, not completely convinced it was the best idea to reject a warm, willing female he knew to be an appealing bed partner, for no other reason than the fact that he'd promised to marry someone he hardly knew. His future bride was a naive young thing who lived like a destitute college student. Not only that, she'd adopted a bird that had unquestionably witnessed more about satisfying a man than her owner could even imagine. "Wendy Isaac," he repeated, noting with regret that his tone was less than elated.

The brunette tapped her foot, her elegantly arched brows dipping in consternation. "Okay, you've said her name. What does that prove?" She planted her hands on her hips. "Tell me this marriage is *not* business, that you love her *wildly. I dare you!*"

He lifted his gaze away from his guest's damning expression. His glance fell on a brass-and-granite table across the room. Atop it, before the window wall, stood a carved wooden stallion, quarter life-size, cantering majestically in a silver stream of moonlight. It crossed Josh's mind that he liked that piece—he supposed—as much as anything in the place. After a moment, his gaze fell once again to the woman before him. Interestingly, he didn't feel as much emotion for Evelyn as he felt for the chunk of wood.

As he looked into angry green eyes, another thought came to him. He liked Wendy Isaac—at least she could make him laugh, and she cared about something besides herself. That had been refreshing to discover about anybody in this day of cynicism and "me first" mentality.

"I'm fond of Wendy Isaac," he stated truthfully. "I'm going to try to be a good husband." He reached for the doorknob, turning it, though his eyes remained on his frowning companion. "Now, if you'll excuse me, Evelyn, I have an early meeting."

The latch clicked and her gaze skittered to the knob.

Josh stepped away, opening the door wide. She stared as though in disbelief, then glared at him. "What was *I*, then?" she demanded.

His polite smile faded as she scowled at him, a mixture of dread and helplessness sparking in her eyes. She looked as though he was holding a gun to her head, and he found himself experiencing a twinge of guilt. She was good at dredging up blame, he had to give her that. The truth was, Evelyn knew what she was to him—and he knew he meant exactly the same thing to her. A diversion. A brief dalliance to satisfy sexual needs. However, he supposed, being the one dumped, she had the right to play "injured party." "Evelyn," he began as gently as he could, "You're a lovely woman, but we both knew—"

A hard slap across his face cut him off. "Don't you dare say it, Josh!" Her features contorted with rage. "Don't tell me what we both *knew!*" Stalking by, she spun on him at the threshold, and lifted her chin belligerently. "I never want to see you again," she shouted. "Don't call me!"

Once she'd flounced out of his line of vision, he closed the door. Frowning, he wondered if her theatrics had been overheard by anyone at this late hour. With a rush of resignation and pity, he stuffed his hands into his trouser pockets. If her face-saving act helped soothe her ego, allowing even one person to think she had broken it off, it was little enough to grant her. After all Evelyn was as much a victim as Wendy, he supposed. He only hoped his new fiancée would never discover how he'd callously manipulated her into a promise of marriage.

He retraced his steps across the living room's plush carpet, heading onto the patio. A shimmering trail of moonlight on the lake caught his eye. Lifting his face to the moon, he scowled. The pale orb stared down at him, its ancient features eerily accusing. "Don't look at me like that," he muttered, rubbing his stinging jaw. "Didn't I turn down a sure thing and get slapped in the bargain, just to remain *honorable?*"

A half dozen tense seconds slipped by as the word "honorable" ricocheted inside his head. Wincing, he turned his back. "Shut up, old man," he snarled. "Who asked you?"

With a despondent sigh, Wendy realized she should have made something easier for dinner, like hot dogs. This menu wasn't working out well. The beef Roulade called for dill pickles. Unfortunately, her shopping list got smudged in the rain, so she'd neglected to buy them. Consequently, she'd been forced to use pickled okra, reasoning that once the thin slices of beef were rolled up around the other ingredients who would know?

But now, witnessing the steaming results of her labors, they didn't look much like the picture in the cookbook. Some of the toothpicks had come out, and their innards lolled on the gravy like shipwreck flotsam in a brown sea.

One of the salad tomatoes ruptured when she stuffed it and looked in need of emergency surgery. Its guts of cooked vegetables poked out the rip in an excruciating-looking display.

At least the apple pudding smelled good. And she'd remembered to buy lemon ice cream for a topping, just as the recipe suggested. She crossed her fingers that the rest of the dinner would taste as good as the apple pudding smelled. She'd been assured by Josh's chef that these were some of his favorite foods. If she was to be his wife, she wanted to show him she cared about such things. She wanted to make him happy he'd chosen *her* over all the women he could have married.

A knock on her door set her heart to beating at the rate of a hummingbird's wings. Hurriedly, she checked her face in the shiny blade of a butter knife. With a self-deprecating giggle she thumped it down on the tile countertop, hoping the rest of her face was as smudge-free as the half-inch strip she'd been able to see.

Nervously she smoothed her yellow cotton dress, fiddling with the collar as she dashed to the door.

"Let's scram! It's the cops!" squawked Al.

Wendy frowned at the crow on her perch as Al flapped her wings and caw-cawed. "Oh, hush," she admonished in a whisper. "Be a good girl, tonight. I have *plans!*" She took a deep breath and threw open the door.

There he was. The man she loved. Every time she saw him, witnessed his masculine perfection, she was gripped in a pleasant paralysis. She trailed her gaze over him, wishing she could devour him, take him completely inside her to keep and hold, to cherish, forever. Dressed casually in beige trousers and a burgundy polo, he looked recklessly elegant, no—he looked too sexy to bear.

"Hi," he said with a grin, his voice releasing her from her immobility.

"Hi, yourself," she echoed breathlessly, running into his arms. His kiss was warm and welcome and she held him close, relishing the feel of his hard chest against her breasts, his subtle scent beneath the tang of cedar-spiced cologne. "I missed you, yesterday," she admitted shyly, her smile and her voice overflowing with love.

He took her hand and drew her inside, closing her door. "Whose fault was that?"

She nuzzled his jaw. "Mine. But it was my day to read stories in the children's ward at the hospital. As for last night, I can't abandon my literacy students, now can I?"

He drew her to the sofa and pulled her down to sit beside him. "Of course not." Releasing her hand, he rested an arm along the back of the sofa. "Besides, I had to meet with—"

"I know," she interrupted with a laugh. "Daddy."

He nodded. "Not my favorite Isaac." He squeezed her shoulders and she reveled in his show of affection. Looking away, he sniffed the air. "What smells so good?"

She took a deep breath. "That's your favorite dessert."

He glanced at her, his brows dipping in incredulity. "Apple pudding?"

She smiled. "I've fixed all your favorites." Unable to help herself, she touched his chin, coaxing him to lower his face. "Because I love you." She lightly kissed his lips, but continued to watch his eyes. They were wonderful eyes, dark, framed by wickedly thick lashes. Yet, something in their depths—

She sat back, suddenly unsure. "Is something wrong, Josh?"

His eyebrows knit for an instant before he recovered, grinning. "Not a thing—except I'm starving." Pushing up, he held out a hand. "Let's eat."

She placed her fingers into his. "Forgive me, sweetheart. Of course, you've had a long day. I'm being selfish."

"Not at all," he countered. "And you shouldn't have gone to all this trouble. My chef could have done this for us. I hope you don't want me to put the poor man out to pasture after we're married. He's only thirty-three.''

''Of course not.'' Wendy curled an arm about his waist. ''But he'll have a day off, won't he?''

''There's the slight chance,'' he kidded.

She laughed. ''And didn't you tell me we'd spend our honeymoon alone at your cabin in the Adirondacks?''

''That's true.'' He glanced down at her, his features amused and curious.

''So, do you cook?'' she teased.

''Actually, I do.'' He chuckled at her surprise. ''So, what are your favorite foods?''

She shook her head. ''Oh, no, a girl has to keep *some* secrets until after the wedding.''

He gave a mock grimace. ''That bad, huh?''

''Certainly not! They're all easy and tasty, but—cholesterol city.'' When they reached the table, she moved his latest bouquet to the side and indicated his place opposite hers. ''You sit and relax. I'll serve.''

Twenty minutes later, Wendy was pleased at how smoothly dinner was going. Josh didn't seem to notice the substituted okra, or at least didn't mention it. And even though his rolled-up beef Roulades all unrolled with an uncharitable lack of consideration for Wendy's painstaking work, they tasted good.

She listened attentively as Josh told her about his day and his plans for rejuvenating her father's company. She watched him dreamily. Could he possibly be even more handsome when he spoke so enthusiastically about the work he loved?

Al landed on Josh's shoulder and nabbed a slice of beef off his fork. After the crow made a fluttery getaway with her booty, Wendy fought a grin at Josh's reaction. For a second he appeared stunned, his fork poised at his mouth. But soon enough his expression eased into a smile. "I realize crows will eat just about anything, but right off my fork?" he quipped. "Is this one of the secrets you were keeping from me until after the wedding?"

"We women of mystery have all kinds of secrets, darling," Wendy joked. "Actually, I think Al wanted a souvenir from you. Be glad she didn't nip out a lock of your hair." Wendy made a pained face. "Trust me. I know what I'm talking about."

He chuckled, and the rich sound sent renewed waves of happiness through Wendy's body. This man, Josh—this love of her life—had a wonderful, deep, sincere laugh. She knew she would never tire of hearing it, not if she lived to be two thousand years old.

Dabbing her lips with her napkin, she inhaled, attempting to slow her heart rate. Every time she looked at him, heard his voice, experienced again that dazzling smile, she went a little batty, wanting to cry out her joy, run madly from housetop to housetop yelling out her bliss.

She'd always been a passionate person—passionate about jumping in and helping people and animals in need—but she'd never felt particularly passionate about a man before. Probably because none of them had been the *right* man. None of them had been Joshua Raven.

Now she knew what her girlfriends meant when they went on and on with gushy exuberance about the special men in their lives. Now she understood how loving a man truly felt. It was one of the most marvelous miracles to be imagined—the divine connection that happened between the right man and the right woman. She felt blessed and humbled to be so fortunate.

Clearing a lump of weepy thankfulness from her

throat, she managed evenly, "Are you ready for dessert? Coffee?"

He winked at her. "You read my mind." He pushed up. "But I'll help. You cooked the whole dinner."

She started to protest, but the woman inside her squelched the urge. She wanted to be near him, to brush against him, to spontaneously kiss and hold the man she loved. To be embarrassingly honest, she was dying for him to sweep the dinner dishes to the floor, grab her up in his arms, throw her on the table and make wild love to her right there.

"What are you looking at?" Josh asked, sounding very near.

She blinked, unaware that she'd slipped into a lewd daydream, lingering there like a demented fool, staring longingly at the table, envisioning their bodies entwined in the act of....

She cast her glance away, unable to look him in the eye for fear he'd see her desire. "Nothing—nothing at all." She flinched at the squeaky sound of her voice, and barreled into the kitchen.

"Something's wrong, Wendy," he insisted, following her.

"No, please." She grabbed a couple of pot holders and opened the oven. Carefully she withdrew the apple pudding, chagrined to see her hands shaking. "I'm being foolish."

When she placed the dessert on the counter, she felt Josh's hands on her shoulders, coaxing her to face him. "Foolish?"

She didn't meet his gaze, but smiled wanly. "Very."

With a finger, he tipped her chin up and she had to look him in the eye. "What could be that foolish?"

She swallowed. She didn't dare tell him she wanted

him to ravish her. It was his place to start the seduction, wasn't it? Or was it okay for a woman to ravish her fiancé if she decided to? She'd never been engaged before. Still, from what she knew of relationships today, men and woman didn't need to be engaged—or even know each other well—to indulge in a little consensual ravishing. Did they?

"What is it, Wendy?" Josh's features closed in confusion. "Have I done something?"

She shook her head at the irony of his question. "No—" She forced a smile, but her cheeks burned. "You haven't done anything...." Those few words were the absolute crux of the problem, yet she sensed Josh wouldn't grasp it. She was being too vague, drat her! Why couldn't she simply grab him by his shirtfront and demand, *"Kiss me!"* like Al did with such mortifying frequency?

"You're a pretty boy! *Kiss me!*" Al screeched, right on cue. Wendy jumped as though her own thoughts had come to life and been bellowed out to humiliate her. Blood thundered in her temples and she was helpless to staunch the flood of emotions that seared through her.

Josh's close scrutiny made her shudder, fearful that he might read her thoughts and think less of her for allowing her feelings to fall to such a base level. She was so ashamed! She'd never had erotic thoughts like this before. It was just—just that she loved him so much. Maybe she was going a little crazy.

Before she knew what was happening she'd thrown herself into Josh's arms and was crying, sobbing. He enfolded her in a tentative embrace, as though perplexed about what was going on, and afraid she might panic if he held her too tightly.

Suddenly it was all too nutty, too surreal, and she had

to laugh. Why should she be ashamed of wanting the man she loved to make love to her? Her laughter mixed with shuddery sobs, making her look completely insane, she knew. But she couldn't help it. She merely clung to Josh, sobbing and hiccuping.

After a minute she was lifted off the ground and carried out of the kitchen. "Wendy, you're overwrought. It's my fault," he assured softly, lowering her to the couch. "I'll go."

When he lifted himself away, she grabbed his wrist. "*No!* I'm not overwrought." She clutched his wrist with both hands. "I'm not crazy, either. I'm just—I just want you to...to..." She swallowed, aware that what she wanted, what she needed from him, was right there for him to see—in her eyes.

He watched her for a moment, his expression bewildered, then compassionate, then cautious. Then uneasy. Anxiety charged through her. Uneasy? Why would a man known as a rake and a playboy be uneasy with the idea of making love to his own fiancée? It made no sense. "Josh?" she cried, frightened, and not sure why.

With her uncertain tone, he blinked, his expression easing into a gentle smile. "I'm sorry, darling. I didn't understand." Lifting her hand he kissed the sensitive pulse point on the inner side of her wrist, murmuring against her skin, "I want you, too, you must know that."

He leaned toward her, bracing a hand beside her head on the cushion. Brushing her hair away from her face, he kissed her cheek, then each eyelid. The touch of his lips was tender, and in its tenderness, unbelievably erotic. "You're the one woman in my life," he vowed softly, his lips trailing sensuously to her mouth. "I want you to be happy." He kissed her then, and the beauty of it brought a hot ache to the back of her throat. She raised her arms to encircle his neck. But all too soon the kiss was over, and a soft cry of longing escaped her lips as he lifted himself away.

"I have something for you, darling," he whispered, taking one more lingering taste of her mouth before he sat up. "I was going to give it to you later this evening, but..." He paused, his expression serious.

All she wanted from him was the gift of his lips on hers, his hands on her bare skin, bringing her alive with his loving. Yet, she couldn't voice her need, could hardly see him. Her eyes were filled with thankful tears—tears that he had read the desire in her eyes, and now knew what to do.

He withdrew something from his trouser pocket and held it out to her. A small black velvet box. "I hope you like it." He lifted her hand, limp and unresponsive, her body still staggered from his kiss.

"A ring?" she asked, startled. *Oh, had she spoiled his romantic seduction with her silly fit?* She hitched up on one elbow. "Open it for me, sweetheart," she urged, in a murmur of wonder.

When he did, she blinked away more tears. Could any woman be this happy? First he would present her with an engagement ring, and *then* he would show her in a very physical way how much he adored her. She stared at the ring, then smiled up at him. "I—I've never seen such a beautiful thing." The diamond was pear-shaped, and nearly as large as her thumbnail. Having been acquainted with many wealthy women over the years, Wendy had seen her share of magnificent diamonds. Even so, this exquisite stone shimmered and flashed with such splendor, it would shame all but a handful of the most spectacular gems.

"May I slip it on your finger?" Josh asked.

She lifted her left hand. "It's lovely," she whispered, though she would have preferred something less splashy. She'd turned her back on her father's showy lifestyle several years ago in favor of a simpler, fuller existence, and such a huge ring made her uncomfortable.

"You don't like it?" he asked.

Wendy's gaze shot to his face. He was more intuitive than she'd imagined. She held it up to look at it, sparkling there on her finger. "Well—it's a little heavy." She gave him a sheepish look. "But—it's from you, Josh, so I love it."

He smiled wryly. "You hate it."

She pushed up to sit, hugging him to her. "I love *you.*" She pulled back to look into his face. "But I'd love you every bit as much if you gave me a simple gold wedding band."

He eyed her curiously. "Are you sure?"

She laughed, loving this vulnerable side to him. "Am I sure I'd love you?" she teased. "Of course, silly. What a question."

"I meant are you sure about the ring?"

"Oh." She stroked his cheek. "I'm sure. Don't be mad."

"Your father might be," he muttered, or at least that's what she thought he said.

"My father?" She shifted to better see him. "Why should we care what he thinks?"

"We don't." He pulled her against him, snuggling her in the crook of his shoulder. "Not at all." He kissed her temple. "One plain, gold band it is." He slid the diamond ring off her finger.

Teasing his throat with her lips, she murmured, "Thank you, sweetheart." She kissed his warm flesh, nipping lightly. His scent was stimulating, arousing her, heightening her senses. Her body fairly hummed with need for him, every fiber of her being eager for the love-making to come. ''You're perfect,'' she whispered through a sigh.

He rested his chin on the top of her head, and she wondered what his expression was—if he smiled with anticipation, too. He held her against him, yet the hand that had removed the ring lay idly by his side, fisted around the jewelry.

''I'm going to leave now, Wendy,'' he said at last.

She blanched, stiffening, not believing what he was saying. Tilting her head back, she stared into his eyes. ''What?''

He removed his arm from around her and stood. Wendy felt cold, though the apartment windows were open, allowing the warm evening breeze inside. She blinked, bewildered. Had she hurt his feelings by refusing his gift? Reaching out, she took his hand. ''Josh, don't go.''

He squeezed her fingers affectionately, but stepped away. ''Things have been moving quickly. I'm to blame. I see now you need a little space.'' He pressed a brief kiss on her forehead. ''I'll call you tomorrow.''

Before she could react, he was gone.

She stared blankly at the door. She *had* hurt him! That little speech about giving her space had been a transparent excuse if she'd ever heard one. Tears welled and overflowed. How stupid could she be? How could she have rejected his ring so bluntly the way she had? She'd called it *heavy* of all things.

He'd taken it as a personal rejection.

Flinging herself down on the couch, she wept into the cushion, calling herself every name she could think of and making up a few, to make sure she didn't misunderstand what a callous ignoramus she was. She'd ruined Josh's beautifully planned seduction, and she'd managed to wound him in the process. No woman in the history of accepting engagement rings could have been as clumsy and unfeeling as she was tonight.

Something poked her in the back as Al hopped to a landing between her shoulder blades.

"Roll me over in the clover!" came a singsong shriek, as the crow sauntered around on her back. "Roll me over in the clover, pretty boy!"

"Oh, Al..." she moaned. "Don't rub it in!"

CHAPTER FOUR

JOSH wasn't accustomed to leaving a woman when she had that "take me" look in her eyes. He wasn't accustomed to driving home with sweat beading his forehead, his knuckles clamped on the steering wheel in sexual frustration. And he wasn't accustomed to taking cold showers while cursing himself for thinking of this marriage as a means to an end—visualizing Gower Isaac's daughter as merely a hostess for business dinners and the mother of his two-point-five children.

He'd never considered how his scheme would affect a flesh-and-blood woman, a woman he was beginning to know as both caring and vulnerable. Yes, all in all, last night had been an evening full of experiences he wasn't accustomed to having, and feelings he wasn't accustomed to feeling.

"Damn."

"Did you say something, Mr. Raven?"

His gaze snapped up to see his secretary pause in the act of laying out his mail. He hadn't heard her come in. He scowled, unable to shake his foul mood. "No. Nothing." He bent over the profit and loss figures he'd been studying, shading his eyes from the young woman. "That will be all for now, Miss Oaks. Just leave the mail."

"Yes, sir."

Though his secretary was an attractive blonde, he made it a point never to get involved with employees. Never to even look at them funny. In today's business climate, if he had an affair with an employee and then dumped her, he would either end up being sued for sexual harassment or he'd come to work one day to find honey and catsup poured in his files. No, thanks. He didn't need female problems at work. That kind of trouble was easy enough to find without asking for it.

He heard the door to his office close and glanced up with a frown. Right now, he was having enough trouble with his fiancée.

Wendy wanted sex.

Maybe it was more correct to say she wanted to be made love to by the man who'd expressed a desire to spend the rest of his life with her. And *blast it,* she had every right to expect that.

He shoved a hand through his hair, slumping back. But he wasn't the man to show her. His one great love had always been his work. That's where he used up his passions every day. Oh, he knew how to seduce a woman and he knew how to please, but to show love? *That,* he didn't know how to do.

Marrying Wendy Isaac under the conditions Gower had outlined was dishonorable enough, without adding insult to injury. Sure, it would be pleasant to have sex with her. She was an attractive woman and he sensed that with the right guidance, she could be an extraordinary lover.

Since she was inexperienced, there was every possibility he could fool her into believing his feelings were more than superficial. But even if he did, taking her to bed before the wedding would be contemptible. She was a decent kid. She deserved to be treated decently.

According to his bargain with Gower, until the wedding vows were spoken, the final papers wouldn't be signed and the stock wouldn't be transferred. So before

Wendy was his legitimate bride, there would be no messing around. He felt like a big enough pile of dirt as it was.

What if something happened and the merger fell through at the last minute? He damn well wouldn't go through with any marriage. And if he walked out, what would it do to an innocent like Wendy to discover she'd given herself so completely to a man who'd been lying to her? A hard fist of disgust twisted his gut, and he tasted bile. *No!* He would not indulge himself sexually simply to satisfy baser needs. Maybe he was a business shark, but he wasn't completely without scruples.

"Okay, smart guy," he grumbled, "how do you plan to keep her in her clothes for the next two months?" Here was yet another experience he was totally unfamiliar with—the *preservation* of a woman's virtue.

Sucking in a quick breath, like someone about to dive into icy water, he closed his eyes. His exhale was slow, through gritted teeth. It was going to be a long two months.

Josh realized with relief that he needn't have worried about keeping Wendy in her clothes. As soon as the news broke in the paper the next morning, it seemed the entire state of Illinois decided to host parties, dinners and showers to celebrate the upcoming nuptials.

Of course most of them were business affairs, and Josh could see that Wendy was only putting up with all the pomp and circumstance for his benefit. She could be a game kid, he mused, watching her smile and chat with the governor and his wife. He lounged against the wall of the country club ballroom where this latest fete was being hosted. Finding a quiet spot amid all the grandeur, glitter and gossip, he simply observed his bride-to-be.

She wore a conservative beige linen dress. The sleeves were short, the hemline falling midway between her knees and ankles. The simple dress had a scooped neck, but not scooped low enough to show cleavage. Her hair was pulled away from her face, not a strand out of place. Her only jewelry was a pair of tiny freshwater pearl earrings. She looked like a young girl at her commencement—a debutante in training.

He had a feeling she'd changed her hairstyle and her mode of dressing for him. It wasn't something he would have asked of her, yet, like learning his favorite foods, she must have assumed he would want her to look more like the cookie-cutter social butterfly her father clearly wanted her to be.

It was odd, but seeing her now, he realized he didn't care for the debutante look on Wendy. She was a "crow in her hair" type of woman, and he found nothing wrong with that. Maybe the world needed more people who weren't afraid to be a little different. He made a mental note to mention that she didn't have to dress for him. Though she was unaware of it, she was doing enough, simply by consenting to be his bride.

He crossed his arms and scanned her face as she laughed. It seemed to him, that even with a string quartet playing Mozart in the background, and the buzz of a hundred guests, he could hear the ring of her laughter. It sounded genuine, and she looked radiant, but Josh knew that deep inside she was upset about having to miss another tutoring session. She'd missed quite a few in the past weeks, not to mention several afternoons reading in the children's ward or taking her turn behind the cash register of the Animal Rescue Thrift Shop.

Still, she never complained. With a sweet smile, she'd said she would make do. She understood the necessity of these things, and after all, it meant so much to Gower. ''Daddy,'' she'd said with a laugh, ''would have a stroke if we declined a single invitation. For once in my life he's proud to call me his daughter.''

Josh dropped his gaze at the memory, clenching his fists in his trouser pockets. Gower didn't deserve Wendy. Neither did he.

''Hey, there, Josh, old man, why are you hiding in the shadows?''

Shifting, he noticed one of his vice presidents grinning at him. ''Just watching my future bride,'' he said, honestly.

''I don't blame you.'' The older man turned to scan Wendy, his expression appreciative. ''She's about as lovely as they come, Josh.'' He shifted back, looking playfully skeptical. ''How'd you ever talk her into marrying a good-for-nothing, workaholic, bum like you?''

Josh grinned wryly at his friend's kidding. ''Luckily, I didn't send you to speak on my behalf, Pete.'' He clamped a hand on the man's shoulder, trying to appear the carefree bridegroom. ''I think I'll go snatch her before the governor says something to make her regret her decision.''

Pete snickered. ''Yeah, weren't you two in college together?''

''That's what I mean.'' Josh pushed away from the wall. ''I was a bit of a womanizer back then.''

''A *bit?*'' Pete chortled. ''Back *then?*''

Josh had taken a step away, but turned back, arching a wry brow. ''I trust your résumé is polished and up to date?''

Pete's laughter didn't fade with the threat. He just waved his boss off.

A moment later Josh joined Wendy. Governor Perry

acknowledged him with a nod, but continued with his story. Since it was one that Josh had heard many times before, he absently observed the crowd. Tucking his fiancée beneath an arm, he tried to communicate his assurance that he understood how hard all this was for her. She responded to his touch with a smile, her bright purple eyes aglow with soft emotions. When she turned back, he watched her profile for a moment before realizing the governor had directed a comment to him. "What?" he finally said, glancing up.

Ben Perry shook his head at his old school friend. "Lovesickness looks good on you, Josh."

He stared at Ben, put off by his analysis. It was interesting how thoroughly people could delude themselves. Just because he'd proposed to Wendy, and because he smiled at her and held her close, people assumed such asinine things. Then again, Ben was easy to bluff. He'd never won a poker game from Josh in his life. Chuckling as though caught, he said, "I could never hide anything from you, could I?"

Ben's grin widened. "Look, it's late. Why don't you two sneak on out? I can tell you'd like to be alone."

Josh sensed Wendy's eyes on him. He glanced at her, feeling trapped. "Would you like to leave, darling?"

She smiled. *Of course she would. Stupid question.* He smiled down at her, though it wasn't easy. He knew what she wanted. *Damn.* Two more weeks until the wedding, and each one of the past six had been tougher than the one before, concocting ways to keep her at arm's length. What was he going to use for an excuse tonight? It was too late for her to believe he was expecting a conference call. Maybe, a headache? He'd tried about everything else. "Well, then...." He glanced at the governor and held out a hand. ''Thanks, Ben. It was nice of you both to do this for us.''

Ben winked. ''It was worth every penny it cost, not to mention the trip up from Springfield. I have to say, I never thought I'd witness the taming of Joshua Raven.'' He took Wendy's hand. ''But then, I'd never met this refreshing woman.''

Wendy flushed. ''Thank you, Governor. And you'll be hearing from me about that literacy legislation when the time comes.''

''I'll look forward to your call.''

The governor stepped away as Mrs. Perry, a petite redhead, gave Wendy a hug. ''Best wishes. I know you two will be very happy.''

Wendy returned the hug, and then faced Josh. ''Ready?'' Her pretty eyes sparkled with anticipation, making Josh more uneasy.

He took her arm, wondering how to stall, yet not appear to be stalling. ''Should we find your father and say goodbye?''

She shook her head. ''He's having a wonderful time. He won't even notice we're gone.''

That was true. Josh had never known any man more egotistical than Gower Isaac. If he could have managed to do the merger and the wedding alone—with neither Josh nor Wendy along to steal any of his thunder—he would have.

The trip to the front door of the country club took ten more minutes, with well-wishers stopping them to visit. Then the parking valet took a few more moments to retrieve Josh's car. *Not nearly enough time,* Josh mused. By one-thirty they were on the road.

Weeks ago, Josh opted to leave his chauffeured limo at home and drive his stick-shift, BMW sports car, for obvious reasons—no back seat, no free hands and a gearshift between their seats, discouraging potential intimacy.

The drive began pleasantly enough, in companionable silence, but that agreeable quiet didn't last long. "Josh?" Wendy asked, her tone sending a jolt though him.

He cast her a quick look. "Yes?"

"Maybe we should spend the night at your place. You have that early meeting, and if you drive me all the way to my apartment, it'll add an hour to your trip.

He watched the highway, trying not to look like he knew this might happen and wasn't crazy about it. If he said he had a headache, she'd definitely not want him to drive all the way to her place. Blast! After a pause, she added, "I've barely seen your apartment—just those two evenings we dropped by between parties. I'd love to spend some time there." She touched his arm, and he stiffened. "Isn't that where we're going to live? At least at first?"

He peered her way, hoping his smile wasn't as stiff as it felt. "I thought we might." Maybe if he avoided the "let's go there and spend the night" part of her question, they'd be beyond the point of no return before it came up again. "I'd think it would be good to stay there for the first year or so. Then, we could look for something in the suburbs, once we decide to start trying to have children."

"I want to start trying right away."

He gritted his teeth and glared at the road. He had to open up *that* can of worms! Where had he thought that remark would lead? Why was he suddenly turning into a mush-brained idiot?

"Josh, please," she said, quietly. There had been no

whining in her request, just the tone of a fiancée who wanted to spend some quality time—naked—with the man she loved. ''Here's the exit for downtown.''

He took the turn, but his brain was working on all cylinders. Was he going to have to burn down the darned high-rise to keep her out of his bed?

She squeezed his arm. ''Good,'' she whispered, and lay her head back. He cast her a surreptitious glance. She'd closed her eyes, and was smiling.

He scowled as he merged into traffic. *Hell, Raven, are you going to be a weak, greedy jerk and take her virginity, or are you going to be strong—reject her again with heaven only knows what excuse—and be a chivalrous, if sexually frustrated, bastard?*

Once inside the apartment, Josh dismissed his butler for the evening. Determined to delay the inevitable, he looked at his fiancée. ''Would you care for anything to drink?''

She shook her head. ''No.'' Coming close, she hugged his middle, lifting her face to invite a kiss. ''I just want you.''

He flinched inwardly, but gave her the kiss she wanted. She held him so tightly he could feel her tremble, her whole body telling him of her need, her passion. He had no problem with the message—at least no problem with the way it was conveyed. She had a nice way with her kisses—innocent, yet full of erotic promises she didn't even know she was making. Yes, she would be an exciting lover.

Oh, no! This was not the way he was supposed to be thinking! His control slipping, he tugged her against him, groaning against her mouth. It had been a hell of a long time between women, and she felt so good. Up to now, he'd been careful with Wendy, very much the gentleman. But it was starting to wear him down. He wasn't accustomed to weeks and weeks of abstinence. And, it seemed, his little fiancée had no plans to make him wait a minute longer.

She drew a handbreadth away and whispered, "Take me to bed, darling."

He wasn't surprised by her request, but he was disheartened by her there-will-be-no-backing-out-tonight expression. If she only knew how badly they both wanted the same thing. He scanned her face, so lovely in expectation.

He hesitated, his physical need battling his wish to be fair. After a few seconds, she surprised him by sliding her arms from around his middle. Almost before he could take a breath, she was standing there in a puddle of linen. He swallowed hard at the sight. She wore nothing but a camisole and tap panties. Pink silk and lace cried out to be slipped lovingly from her comely body.

With a sinking feeling, he gaped at her, so ripe and ready, so willing to be loved. His mouth felt like old parchment. She stood, proud, vulnerable, with her heart wide open to him. *Oh, Lord!* He closed his eyes. A groan of frustration, like the growl of a wounded beast, escaped his lips.

"Where's your bedroom?" He felt her hand grip his with determination. "Show me."

He stared at her, so exquisite, so resolved to have her virginity taken away. Wasn't this scenario every man's fantasy? Her eyes remained on his, innocently questioning, coaxing, and once again he was assailed by weakness and yearning. Inclining his head he indicated the direction. "Back there," he rasped.

She smiled, drawing him along in her wake. She was all pale skin and liquid grace, the pain in Josh's gut was so severe he had trouble walking upright. Hellfire, was he sure waiting was a good idea, after all? Maybe it would be better to.... *Damn!* He shook off the rationalization. *If you do this, Raven, you're nothing but a lecherous predator!*

They entered his bedroom, made golden by hidden accent lighting. A king-size bed dominated the masculine room. Sheers covered the window wall, giving them gauzy access to a sky full of stars and the vast Lake Michigan, forty stories below.

Wendy led him to the bed, where she sat down, kicking off her high-heeled sandals. "I like the room. It even smells like you." Her smile seemed exactly like that of the Mona Lisa—vaguely sensual, yet shy.

A deep ache wrenched his belly as she drew him down to sit beside her. He felt guilty and selfish—all too aware that he was losing the last remnants of control. He faced the fact that he had to do something drastic, right now, or Wendy would find herself flat on her back beneath him, her underwear ripped from her, their bodies writhing with pent-up desires.

He pushed himself off the bed, jamming his hands into his pockets. He couldn't stand to look into those big, hopeful eyes. "Wendy," he began roughly, "this is hard for me, but I have to tell you..." He had no idea what he was going to say. Maybe he could make up something about how it was a family tradition not to touch his fiancée before marriage. Would she swallow that, knowing his reputation? Would she believe it if he assured her that some women were worthy of marriage and some only for playing around, and she was... *No, blast it!* He didn't even believe that one. Perfectly saintly women lost their virginity before they were married, every day. So what the hell was he going to—

"I know everything, Josh," she cut in so quietly he wasn't sure he heard her say it.

He frowned, facing her. "What?"

She pulled up on her knees and took his hand, forcing him to sit. "I said, I know everything." She took his face between her hands.

He eyed her with caution. *She knew everything?* "You do?" he asked, warily. If she knew everything, then why was she wearing pink, lacy underwear, holding his face tenderly? Why wasn't she driving a stake through his heart?

Wendy nodded, looking solemn. "I began to suspect that night I fixed you dinner in my apartment, but I didn't want to believe it."

He became increasingly apprehensive under her grave scrutiny, even though there was no place in her skimpy attire to conceal a weapon. He decided he'd better go along and try to figure out what she thought she knew. "You didn't?" he stalled, fishing for clues.

She nodded again, drawing up and kissing his lips with great care, as though she feared he might break. "And since I volunteer at the library once a week, I've been reading up on it."

It? What the hell was *it?* He had no idea what she could have been reading up on—unless it was *The Scheming, Manipulative Male Monster and How To Make Him Suffer*? If so, she was off to a fantastic start in that outfit. "You have?"

She sat back on her heels, her expression tender. "And don't you worry, impotence is nothing to be ashamed of."

He heard her, but he couldn't believe his ears. "Impo—*what?*"

She leaned forward and hugged him, her breasts soft

against his back. "It's the stress—of the merger. You're working so hard—seven days a week, ten hours a day—and then you have to put up with all these social things at night." Her breath caressed his ear. "I, above all people, know how Daddy can be. Darling, I'm not surprised you're—having problems."

He eyed the ceiling. Lord! Impotence? This was an excuse he never would have thought of. Men didn't even like to be in the same room with *that* word. The idea was so ludicrous it was funny. He pursed his lips, trying to squelch a wayward grin.

When he turned to look at her face, tears trembled on her lower lashes. Good Lord, had she been that upset? Evidently, she'd been worrying silently for weeks. About him. All thoughts of laughter drained away. He couldn't recall ever seeing anyone look at him like that. Not since he was eight years old. He'd been riding a rickety old bike and was hit by a drunken driver. His arm had been broken in three places and he'd had a bad concussion. When he woke up in the hospital, his mother's eyes had glimmered with tears just that way.

Unable to think of a thing to say, he kissed her cheek. The act was spontaneous, and he wasn't sure what brought it on. Possibly it was because she'd come up with this justification for not taking her to bed—however bizarre. Or possibly it was because the whole idea that she'd been reading up on such a delicate topic—trying to help—was extraordinarily kind.

She lifted up and forward enough to reach his lips with hers and kissed him back. The sweet sensuality of the act reawakened his male ardor, and he was grateful she was pressed against his back. "I'm sure when we're off by ourselves on our honeymoon I can get you all relaxed and you'll be fine," she whispered.

He exhaled heavily. *You keep kissing me like that and the last thing I'll be is relaxed,* he groused inwardly.

When he realized she was about to kiss him again, he looked away in self-defense. "It's good of you to take it this way, Wendy." He hated to have to go along with this, but he had to admit, it was a godsend, and just in time.

"Let me lie next to you tonight, Josh. Hold you." She wrapped her arms about him again, her breasts burning cruelly into his back. "I don't want to put any pressure on you. Just be with you. Okay?"

He stirred restively, trying to overcome his arousal. He cleared his throat. "Of course—that would be nice." What could he say? No? After all her worry, her *study*—on his behalf? The word "impotence" forced its way into his mind and he winced, wondering if other volunteers at the library noticed her area of interest.

She released him with a brief kiss above his shirt collar. "I'll let you get ready for bed, darling."

He felt the bed move. When he turned to look at her, he saw the flash of a shapely leg as she slipped beneath the covers. When she smiled at him, he lifted his chin in a half nod and got up before he did something really stupid and counterproductive.

Since he didn't wear pajamas, and under the circumstances suspected nudity was not the best idea, he scrounged up a pair of baggy cotton shorts. Once he crawled into bed, she was immediately cuddling in the crook of his arm, hugging him close. "Good night, sweetheart," she said. "I love you."

He kissed her, but just barely, not wanting to start anything he couldn't keep himself from finishing. "Good night," he whispered, staring up at the ceiling.

Hours later Josh still stared at the ceiling. She didn't

want to put any pressure on him, he mused ironically. Her body rubbing against his was certainly no pressure. *No pressure at all.* Yeah, right! He had a meeting with his board of directors in two hours and he'd done nothing but stare at the ceiling trying not to feel her soft curves molded against him, trying not to inhale the sweet scent of her hair.

The hand that hugged his chest for hours had slipped lower, and was now below the waistband of his shorts. Any further slippage and Wendy would awaken with a very big shock, and the realization that her fiancé was not quite the stress-impaired man she thought he was.

Gently, he lifted her hand to a safer spot on his chest. Stroking her fingers absently, he wondered how he'd gotten himself into such a weird situation. Wendy Isaac was a unique little bird. He'd never run across a woman like her. She threw herself into everything she did with her whole being—including loving a man, it appeared. She seemed to love him, completely, uncompromisingly, even when she thought he was—well, amorously impaired. He didn't know any women who would do what she was doing—just hold him as though the strength and depth of her love could heal him.

He looked at her, sleeping so soundly and peacefully. So trusting.

She was nice, dammit. He nuzzled her hair, then found himself kissing the top of her head.

She stirred, a fragile sigh warming his throat, and he drew her closer. When he realized he'd instinctively folded her into his arms, he frowned. Confused, he lifted his gaze to the ceiling.

Was it possible, he pondered, *that pure, unqualified love, given so selflessly, might be a little bit catching?*

CHAPTER FIVE

JOSH agreed completely with Wendy about her father's absurd idea of what her wedding should be. Ostentatious was the mildest adjective that came to mind for the ceremony that included every fatuous excess imaginable, from twelve trumpeteers, costumed like palace guards, to the harp quartet, decked out to resemble angels.

Wendy had wanted to be married among a few close friends on the patio of her mother's ancestral home, but Gower put his foot down. His daughter's marriage to the wealthy and powerful Joshua Raven would be the event of the season. How dare Wendy even consider depriving him of this social opportunity?

Josh had wanted to flatten the man then and there, but he'd kept silent. The wedding ceremony was the bride's family's domain. Besides, Josh had enough on his plate running his own company as well as finalizing plans for refurbishing Gower's holdings—once he was officially CEO.

Still, no matter how surreal and absurd the wedding was, Josh didn't think Wendy had been tainted by the excesses. As she stood beside him, in flowing white, before the minister, he thought she looked—well, like a fairy princess. Her huge, purple eyes glimmered engagingly as she repeated her vows.

When his turn came, Josh faced the minister to hear the holy words that spoke of loving, honoring and cherishing his bride—until death. His "I do" rang clearly, echoing in the cavernous cathedral. Inwardly, he winced, hoping his pledge to love her would not prove to be a lie. Closing his eyes, he silently swore he would try his best.

''You may kiss the bride.'' The minister's voice broke through Josh's grim contemplation, startling him. The end of the ceremony? So soon? It was amazing how few moments it took to bind two people to each other for life. Grateful for the small favor of short Protestant weddings, he turned toward his new wife. Lifting her veil, he gave her the traditional kiss. Her lips trembled, and he tasted salty tears. Confused, he pulled slightly away. ''Are you all right?''

She smiled. ''I'm so happy.''

A jolt shot through him. She was crying with *happiness?* Even after all the browbeating her father had put her through in order to use her wedding for his own selfish purposes? Genuinely touched by her forgiving nature, he grinned. If it had been left up to him, he would have told the old goat to go to Hades and let Wendy get married the way she wanted to.

Josh leaned down, kissing her again, this time with greater fervor. He could feel her fingers tentatively touch his waist and he knew she wanted to squeeze him hard, hold him tightly. Love him. And dammit, he had the same urge.

She'd taken to sleeping beside him every night, hugging his middle. It had been a rough two weeks, but he'd managed to suffer her gentle touch without so much as an audible groan of lust. By now he was teetering on the edge of sanity, his desire to drag her to the floor and take her right there, difficult to deny.

Fortunately, decorum prevailed. After enjoying the taste of her kiss for a few more seconds, he ended it. Then, accompanied by traditional organ music, Josh escorted his bride down the isle and out of the packed sanctuary.

A million pictures and a trillion handshakes later, they made it to the site of the reception and dinner. Gower had rented the ballroom in one of Chicago's most palatial country clubs, where he had been a long-time member. Josh had never joined any clubs. Since he didn't play golf or care that much for society life, he'd opted to restrict his associations to work.

Accompanied by background music of a twenty-piece orchestra, the festivities seemed to grind on forever. Gower played the effusive master of ceremonies, everlastingly popping up to make wordy toasts, or pontificate about the meaning of life and the importance of love. Considering what Josh had learned from Wendy about the man's loveless marriage to Wendy's mother, Josh knew Gower's indulgence into pseudo-philosophic prattle was wholly for the sake of hearing his own voice.

Josh ground his teeth. He should have sensed Gower would milk the occasion for every scrap of attention he could get. Compared to that old tyrant, he felt like a novice in the art of manipulation. Which was ludicrous, considering the major-league tampering he'd done to Wendy's life.

After the congratulatory speeches were finally over, Wendy leaned close, drawing Josh from his irascible thoughts. "How are you?" she whispered.

Though his mood was far from cheerful, he couldn't help but smile. She was obviously concerned about his physical problem, or what she *thought* was his problem. Could he blame her? After all, she was about to leave on her honeymoon. He covered her hand with his and squeezed. "I'm only anxious about one thing—and that's how long it will be before I can get you alone."

Her cheeks flushed. Strange, but he never seemed to tire of seeing that. As the orchestra switched from classical selections to a more danceable tune, Josh looked at his watch, wondering how much longer this silliness would go on. They had a long trip ahead of them if they were going to get to his place in the Adirondacks tonight. "Our flight's in two hours," he said in an aside to Wendy. "We need to go fairly soon."

Wendy smiled. "You won't get any arguments from me, darling."

Gower came up to his daughter, his features florid. He looked puffed up with pride, but Josh didn't think Wendy was fooled. He was only full of himself—portraying the devoted daddy with melodramatic zest. "It's time to get the dancing started, daughter." With a flourish he took her hand. "I believe the first dance is traditionally mine."

Gower squeezed Josh's shoulder, drawing his gaze. The older man briefly nodded, murmuring something. With the swell of the melody, Josh couldn't hear. He felt a prick of misgiving and wondered if Gower had been affirming that the wedding made their merger a done deal. He frowned, appalled, as the fairy princess was led away by the egocentric old troll. "Don't say anything, you idiot," he grumbled. "Especially not in front of your daughter."

Gower's self-absorption was disgusting. Didn't the man ever spare a thought to Wendy's feelings? Didn't he remember or care that his daughter wasn't supposed to know about the marriage deal? One wrong word at the wrong time, and she would be shattered. Josh might not be in love with her in the head-over-heels sense, but he cared about her. The last thing he wanted was to see her hurt.

Gower swirled his daughter onto the dance floor, showing himself off as Mr. Perfect-Father-And-Expansive-Host. It was all Josh could do to look pleasant. Unfortunately, Gower's self-importance wasn't the only thing making him irritable. Evelyn Jannis was there, sitting a table away. He felt a tug of regret but not surprise when she stood and wriggled his way. He smiled politely but eyed her as though she were a coiled rattlesnake.

She placed a hand on his. "Hello, sweets."

"I didn't expect to see you, Evelyn," he said with as little edge to his voice as he could manage.

"I came with Daddy." She lifted a shoulder in a casual shrug. "Surely you knew he and Gower are old poker buddies."

"I didn't know." When her smile broadened—a clear indication she thought he was lying, that she believed the wedding invitation meant *he* wanted her there—his grip on politeness slipped to dangerous levels. "Well, Evelyn," he began, thin-lipped, "it's been nice seeing—"

"You look yummy in that tux, sweets," she broke in, her grin sly. "I could eat you up."

He pursed his lips, biting back an unchivalrous remark. "I know what you can do, Evelyn." Removing his hand from hers, he went on. "However, this is hardly the time or place to—"

"Okay, sweets," she interrupted, perching a hip on the table. "Call me when you get back. We'll find a time and place." She cast a glance at Wendy and her father, the sole couple on the dance floor. "You know my number."

He scanned her, ravishing, sleek and completely amoral. Evelyn Jannis was any lecherous bachelor's idea of a great date. "I'm trying to forget your number," he muttered, unsettled that he'd responded with such naked honesty.

Her expression grew cunning. "Trying?" She trailed a fingernail across his knuckles. "That's the most interesting remark I've heard in ages." She stood, but leaned down, displaying ample cleavage. "You keep *trying,* sweets." With a shrewd twitch of her lips, she added, "And when you fail, I'll be there."

She walked away, but her perfume lingered. Josh felt an absurd guilty twinge, as though he'd been caught with lipstick on his collar. Blast! He didn't want to be attracted to Evelyn, or any old girlfriend. He wanted to be attracted to his wife. And he was.

But would he still be after his lust was satisfied? Was what he felt for Wendy anything more substantial than frustrated animal need? Could he keep his promise to be the husband she deserved? He exhaled long and low, recalling with a stab of guilt all he was gaining with the marriage. After a few moments of internalized counseling—reminding himself that today he had made a commitment to Wendy, in good faith—he looked up to see his wife and her father finish their dance. He felt almost slime-free.

Almost.

After the music ended, Gower swaggered back with Wendy displayed on his arm like a prize cockatoo, handing her over to Josh. "Your dance, I believe—*son.*"

Josh stood. Taking Wendy's hand, he led her onto the dance floor then drew her into his arms as another waltz commenced. "After this, we're out of here," he grumbled near her ear. "I've had all I can stomach."

"I'm with you. Five more minutes of being paraded

around like a prize sow at the state fair and I'll start screaming.''

He chuckled. ''Speaking of screaming and calling out, are you sure you want to take Al along?''

Wendy's smile dimmed. ''Why—don't you?''

He felt like a rat. He hadn't meant to toss cold water on any of her plans. She'd had enough of that done to her by her father. ''It's fine with me. I just thought she'd be happier with Millville.''

Wendy shook her head. ''She's been lonely a lot lately—barking herself hoarse. I hate to leave her where Daddy might upset her.''

Josh lifted a knowing brow. ''Right. We wouldn't want to come back and find her stuffed and mounted in your father's den.''

Her big eyes grew bigger. ''Horrors.'' Recovering her smile, she added, ''She's waiting at my apartment. I've never seen her so excited. And we have to go there to get my bags and change, anyway.''

He laughed. ''Okay, okay. I'd hate for it to get out that I refused my bride's request to take an extra female on my honeymoon. Very kinky, but for *you,* I'll do it.'' He led her in a spin as the music faded. ''I'll race you to the car.''

She squeezed his hand, lovingly. ''Let me say good-bye to my friends.''

He allowed her to lead him to the table where her volunteer cronies and literacy students had been seated. If it bothered her that they'd been hidden away at a faraway table near the kitchen, she didn't show it.

Josh had been introduced to them in the reception line, but he couldn't recall which ones volunteered where—except for a couple of library volunteers, whose sympathetic looks had made him want to grab them by the shoulders and insist he was *not* having manhood problems. Nevertheless, considering the circumstances, he simply smiled and gritted his teeth.

As they approached the table, Josh realized this small group of ten people were subtly dissimilar from the rest of the guests. Dressed suitably, but unlike so many of the other guests, these people lacked gaudy pretensions. Not a ten-carat diamond ring or tie tack in the bunch. Yet, Josh recognized the names of one or two, and knew them to be quite well off. These people were fundamentally different from most of the people he knew. No doubt the difference was that they cared for things other than themselves. And it showed. That difference showed in their eyes and their smiles. That was what set the table apart, really. An aura of basic goodness.

This friendly, caring band of individuals would have been nearly all the wedding guests, if Gower had given his daughter her way. And considering what they had been put through today, Josh would have preferred that, too. These people might not make headlines on the society pages, but they were every bit as genuine and worthy as Wendy. He was sorry he hadn't had more time to get to know them. He had a feeling they were the sort who would be there for a friend in need. Like Wendy had been there for him these past few weeks—giving her all and asking nothing in return.

Josh watched his wife as she gave each one at the table a hearty hug, promising to see them in two weeks. Taking Wendy's cue, Josh shook the men's hands and accepted brief hugs from the women. The two library volunteers seemed to squeeze harder, as though trying to dispense strength—so he could perform his husbandly duties. Or was it a stupid impression he'd conjured up in his own head? *He damn well hoped so.*

After making his own farewells to a few close buddies, Wendy tossed her bouquet to a writhing knot of squealing females. An attractive mahogany-skinned literacy volunteer caught the bouquet.

"Karen Ann!" Wendy cried.

Squealing with joy, Karen Ann sprang into the air, wriggling and high-kicking, like a quarterback doing a victory dance in the end zone after a touchdown. Her impromptu performance was so free-spirited and whimsical, even Josh joined in the laughter and clapping.

"I gather she's happy," Josh shouted over the noise.

Wendy grinned. "I don't see her live-in boyfriend remaining single much longer," she shouted. "If Karen Ann aims one of her high kicks at him, he'll either instantly promise to marry her or she'll put him in a coma."

As the melee died down, the newlyweds were free to make their escape. Josh noticed that Gower hadn't advanced to receive a kiss from his daughter, or to offer a goodbye hug. She lingered by the door, watching him. When he made no move to come to her, she gave a tentative wave.

It was apparent that Gower was so busy glad-handing with the governor, he hardly had time to acknowledged their departure. His answering wave was more like an impatient dismissal. The old man had gotten all he wanted from both his daughter and son-in-law, and had more important social and political fish to fry.

With a stab of aggravation, Josh took Wendy's arm and pulled her outside. Though she smiled at him, he bore witness to the flash of distress in her eyes. That tiny melancholy shimmer made it clear that she'd thought her acquiescence to Gower's every wish might have softened him towards her. Oh, she was good at hiding her hurt. She covered well, making jokes about her father. Still it was painfully evident that, like most daughters, Wendy would have loved to be close to the man who had given her life.

Josh forced from his mind pleasant visions of dismembering Gower and murmured, "Come on—*Mrs.* Raven."

The happy flush of her cheeks charmed him so much he kissed the tip of her nose. Closing her door, he strode around the car to get in on the other side. He might not be "in love" the way the songs described it, but Wendy Isaac Raven was a sweet, passionate woman. And by heaven, he swore by all the work he'd done to secure this merger, that *nothing* would screw up this honeymoon!

Wendy didn't quite know what she thought would happen when she and Josh got to her apartment—maybe a quick, fiery bout of lovemaking on her rug, quenching their thirst for each other so they could relax on the flight to New York.

As it all too frequently happens with fantasies, that's not the way it worked out.

When they reached Wendy's apartment, her neighbor, Judy Sawyer, was waiting for them. Judy was a quiet young woman, a single mother struggling to make a life for herself and her five-year-old son, Seth. The thin, sweet-faced woman wore faded jeans and a green tank top. Looking bashful, she held out a brightly wrapped package.

"I hated to miss the wedding," Judy said. "Seth has that stomach flu that's going around. But rather than pout about missing your wedding, I spent the time working on my court reporter skills. I have that job interview coming up.'' She grinned shyly. ''It wasn't as much fun as the wedding, I'm sure.''

Wendy liked Judy and her son, and knew that becoming a court reporter would give them a more secure financial footing. Even if Seth weren't sick, Wendy would have understood if Judy had missed the wedding to study. ''I understand.'' Wendy smiled, accepting the gift. ''When I get the pictures back, I'll come by. Okay?''

Judy nodded, appearing grateful. ''You look so beautiful,'' she murmured, her glance shifting to Josh.

He grinned. ''Thank you. I don't think I've ever been called beautiful before.''

Judy blushed. ''Well, you're beautiful, too, but I was talking to Wendy.''

''Story of my life,'' Josh kidded, with a laugh.

As he unlocked Wendy's door, Judy began to gather up the flowing train. ''Your dress is so wonderful,'' she said in awe. ''It must have been like a fairytale.'' She followed them inside the apartment, then lovingly spread out the train, gazing at it like a little girl in the presence of royalty. Wendy noticed a wistful sheen in Judy's blue eyes. No doubt she was thinking about her own husband, who died when Seth was two. Silently Wendy wished Judy well—that she would get the job as a court reporter and find another man to love as thoroughly and completely as Wendy loved Josh.

It suddenly occurred to Wendy that she was still holding Judy's gift. It would be impolite not to open it while Judy was there. ''Oh—your present.'' She untied the ribbon, glancing at Josh. He watched her, his eyes twinkling. She smiled, wondering if he'd had the same fantasies of a torrid indulgence before catching the plane. From his expression it seemed he had, and he, too, could see the chance of that happening quickly disappearing. At least he took the realization with gracious good humor. Josh Raven was a wonderful, gallant, giving man!

Wendy tore away the silver wrappings and set the box on the sofa. Lifting the lid, she found a quart jar amid the tissue.

"It's an old family recipe for marshmallow mint sauce," Judy explained. "Tastes wonderful on ice cream or chocolate pudding." Her thin cheeks glowed red. "It may not seem like much of a gift, but in my mother's family it's become a wedding tradition. For good luck. If you eat it on your honeymoon, you'll have a deliriously happy married life." Her smile grew melancholy. "If Seth's daddy hadn't gotten sick and..." She swallowed hard. "Well—we were deliriously happy, Jerry and I. For the six years we had together."

A lump formed in Wendy's throat, and her nose tickled, a sure sign she was going to cry. Handing the jar to Josh, she hugged Judy. "How sweet of you," she whispered. "That's the most thoughtful gift I can think of. Thank you." With a sisterly kiss on Judy's cheek she backed away.

When she focused on Judy's face, her neighbor was blinking back tears, too. "You'll let me know the instant you get that court reporter job, you hear?" Wendy insisted, her voice shaky with emotion. "I'll be holding a good thought."

Judy nodded, wiping away a tear. "Yes—and, well..." She cast a shy glance at Josh. So did Wendy. He watched Judy with compassion, his smile gone. "I wish you both all the happiness in the world," Judy went on, backing away. "I—I guess you need to get ready, huh?"

Josh nodded and held up the jar. "While Wendy changes, I'll pack this." He winked. "Thanks."

Tall and lean in his tux, Josh looked more princely at that moment than she could ever remember. His expression genuinely sympathetic, his eyes gentle, Wendy's heart swelled with love.

With a wave, Judy made a quick exit. The young woman was dear, and her son was a sweet, timid child. Wendy would miss being their neighbor.

"I'll have Higgins put this in my duffel," Josh said, drawing her back.

Going up on tiptoes she kissed his jaw. "You're sweet to want to take it along."

His brows came up as though in surprise. "What? And fly in the face of tradition?"

She giggled, slipping her arms about him. "I love you so much, darling."

He tenderly drew her against him. With a sigh that sounded as ripe with frustration as she felt, he kissed her temple. "Go get changed—before I do something rash."

She knew what he meant. She had an urge to act very rashly, too, but she reluctantly withdrew from the harbor of his embrace. "I'm going." This was best—not succumbing to something rushed and fevered. It was terribly chivalrous of Josh to want her first experience to be wonderful, meaningful—with plenty of time to linger and savor each other, without impediments like time schedules or—or chauffeurs! Even though they could draw the curtain in Josh's limousine, she would feel uncomfortable with Higgins up front *knowing!* She imagined Josh felt that way, too, for the problem had never come up.

"I'll change out here." He indicated the bag he'd brought containing his travel clothes. "I don't trust myself to keep my hands off you otherwise."

With great effort she turned away from the delicious man she'd married. ''I'll hurry,'' she said, taking extra care to keep her voice even. ''We wouldn't want to miss the plane and ruin our honeymoon.''

His hearty laughter chased her into her room. It wasn't until she'd closed her door that she realized what his laughter meant. The steamy vision that slammed into her brain made her body go hot with anticipation. He was telling her that even if they ended up *walking* to the Adirondacks their honeymoon would be a blissful success. Joshua Raven—her fully functional husband—would see to that!

Nothing—absolutely *nothing* on this earth or in heaven could spoil the perfection of her happiness.

CHAPTER SIX

JOSH could see the lights of Raven's Roost from the cruiser's cabin. At last. He checked the illuminated dial of his wristwatch. Nearly two in the morning. The trip, by plane, hired car, then boat, to his isolated hideaway in the Adirondacks, had been long and tiring.

He glanced at Wendy. She was curled up on a cushioned bench, her face turned toward the bulkhead. She'd fallen asleep almost as soon as the cabin cruiser left the dock. He smiled at her, leaning down to touch her shoulder. "Darling, we're here." He watched her profile as she stirred.

When she shifted to look up at him, she blinked as though she wasn't sure she was awake. Then she smiled. "Hi." The greeting sounded charmingly sleepy, and had a sensual effect on him.

He put out a hand in a wordless offer to help her to her feet. "Ready?"

Her shy smile said it all.

Moments later their bags and Al's covered cage had been removed from the boat by the two-man crew and placed inside the door to their honeymoon retreat. The pine log dwelling had been stocked with food and readied for them, per his secretary's instructions. An array of lights had been left on, emitting a welcoming glow. As Josh and his bride hurried hand in hand up the winding granite-slab path toward the house, Josh heard the boat's motor rev. He glanced back to watch it set about for a return trip to civilization, wondering if he should have told them to check back next Saturday, rather than leaving them alone for two whole weeks. Well, it was too late to worry about that now. Shifting back, he noticed Wendy was watching him. He smiled at her, hoping his hesitation hadn't shown on his face.

After they mounted the stairs that led to a broad covered porch, Josh stepped inside, holding the door for Wendy. Her dawdling made him glance at her face, puzzled. "What's wrong?"

Her smile was bashful and she cast her gaze down. "I thought—I thought you might carry me over the threshold."

He felt like a fool. He was married, after all, and carrying one's new bride inside their honeymoon home was a time-honored tradition. With a quick grin, he quipped, "Already bossing me around, hmmm?" He winked to make sure she realized he was joking.

Before she could respond, he lifted her into his arms, carrying her into the rustic entry hall. "Your neighbor Judy doesn't have the only family with venerated honeymoon traditions."

Wendy hugged his neck and giggled. "And this one doesn't even have calories."

"We aim to please," Josh teased.

"Promises, promises." She nuzzled his cheek. "And don't think I won't hold you to that."

He gazed fondly at her. Those big, purple eyes were wide now. Not a trace of sleep in them. He inclined his head and she met him halfway. Her lips were warm against his, a tantalizing invitation, as she clung to him. The small sound of desire that issued up from her throat had its effect, and he lost any urge to joke around. When the kiss ended, he was no longer smiling. "There's another tradition that takes place on honeymoons—hopefully on the wedding night—that's venerated, too."

She met his glance steadily. "Really?"

He nodded. She was cute, looking so flushed and wide-eyed. He had an impulse to sweep her straight up the stairs and into bed. But he fought it. Honeymoons with inexperienced brides shouldn't be rushed. He didn't want to scare her.

She snuggled against him. "Would you like me to guess what that other tradition is?"

"Go ahead." Her kittenish seductiveness caused a new swell of heat to rush through him. He could dive into those lovely eyes and cheerfully drown.

"I have no idea," she teased with a smile. "But if you'll put me down, I'll show you what I *think* it might be."

Visions of the night two weeks ago surged in his memory—when she'd stepped out of her dress, all willing and vulnerable. That time he'd been bound by honor not to touch her, but nothing would keep him from enjoying her charms tonight. He set her on her feet. "Show me," he said, his voice strangely hoarse.

Her smile was teasing as she walked to his duffel. Her loafers pit-a-patted almost coquettishly across the parquet.

"What are you doing?" he asked, knowing she couldn't possibly tug anything sheer and sexy from *his* bag.

"You'll see." She slipped the latches. "Be patient."

I've been patient for two months! he said inwardly, grinning at her playful tantalizing. For an inexperienced young woman, she knew how to titillate.

"Here." She turned to display her prize. "Marshmallow mint sauce!"

He stared. This wasn't what he'd had in mind at all. "You're kidding."

She stood and moved to him, taking his arm. "Show me the kitchen. We must have some for luck. Remember?"

He chuckled. "I don't think we were required to eat it the instant we got here."

She eyed him with impish determination. "Kitchen?"

He shook his head, grunting out a low laugh. "I suppose we get no further with this honeymoon until we've had some?"

"You suppose correctly, Mr. Raven."

He indicated the living room ahead of them. "Through there, Mrs. Raven." They descended two steps to a large room with walls of whole pine branches and big windows. As they wended their way around cushioned, log furniture, he said, "I don't think we have any ice cream or pudding."

"Minor details." She passed him a sweet smile. "Besides, I'm not that hungry."

They reached another foyer, this one smaller and devoid of furniture. A sliding-glass door gave access to an interior courtyard with an enclosed shade garden. A bubbling central fountain was subtly lit.

Josh led Wendy on around a corner into a beamed dining room, the wood ceiling fitted with tongue-and-groove pine. Skirting the oval table, he directed his wife through a pantry bulging with food stuffs. At last, they entered an airy, picturesque kitchen, constructed of more natural pine. Above a work island, in the center of the room, hung a wrought-iron pot-hanging rack, overflowing with polished copper cooking vessels.

"Will this do?" he asked, releasing her arm.

She scanned the place, her expression filled with wonder. ''The whole house is amazing! Beautiful!'' Facing him, she added in hushed awe, ''I thought you said it was a cabin. This is huge.''

He felt a strange sense of gratification at her compliment. Somehow her approval made the house seem more appealing than he'd ever thought before. The simmering passion in his belly leaped to flame and he battled down a mighty urge to toss her to her back onto the table. Instead, he took the sauce jar from her fingers and with one mighty twist removed the lid. ''Now what?''

She looked at the jar he held out, then at his face. Her expression of love was encouraging, yet a blush colored her cheeks—a devilishly arousing combination. He wondered if her belly sizzled, too. He doubted it. Virgins didn't sizzle until they learned what to sizzle about.

Reaching into the jar with two fingers, Wendy scooped at the beige stuff, then surprised him by holding them up to his lips. ''You first.''

He cocked his head, eyeing her. ''This isn't what I had in mind for two in the morning.''

She pressed her sauce glazed fingers to within an inch of his mouth. ''*Eat.* I want to be made love to.''

Her blunt addendum surprised and tickled him. He didn't plan to argue *that.* Taking her fingers into his mouth, he sucked the sweet, minty sauce from her, teasing her flesh with his teeth. With her startled inhale, he grasped her wrist so she couldn't reflexively remove her hand. With deliberate thoroughness, he licked away sauce that had dripped along her palm.

''Ummm.'' Pulling her two fingers back into his mouth, he suckled, watching her face as she stared. Barely suppressing a grin, he followed another dribble down her palm, kissing and licking as he went. All the while, he eyed her face. Her lips sagged open in a small "oh."

He nibbled and stroked, casually indulging himself with the sweet taste of her skin until he reached the inside of her wrist. Sliding his tongue back and forth, back and forth, in a light caress, he ended his pilgrimage by kissing the sensitive flesh.

When he released her arm, she didn't move. Didn't drop her hand, and her breathing had become rapid and faint. Apparently his uninitiated little bride had never been made aware of the erotic potential of food. She simply gaped at him, her arm bent upward, hand flopped forward.

Suddenly there were no shadows across his heart. He was extremely gratified that he was here—on his honeymoon.

With her.

He burned to make love to her, to teach her the earthly, intimate pleasures a man and woman could share. Scooping up a finger full of sauce, he held it to her lips, still sagging open in the astonished "oh." "Your turn."

She blinked, then blinked again, seeming to return slowly from her dazed state. "What?"

Leaning close, he waved the marshmallow-mint-sauced finger in front of her eyes. "For luck, remember?" he murmured, charmed by her struggle to recover.

When she only stared, he touched her upper lip with the gooey stuff and observed the pleasant sight as she licked it away with her tongue.

As he watched, her lips curved into a smile. She grasped his wrist and pressed his finger inside her mouth. Her gaze holding his, she licked his finger as he'd done, then teased with her teeth.

He swallowed as her mouth moved against his palm to catch a few droplets, her tongue stroking. She nipped at the fleshy part of his palm, below his thumb, teasing and exciting with her tongue.

He cleared his throat. She was doing fine, this inexperienced bride of his. ''Wendy,'' he groaned, tugging from her grasp. ''It's time we satisfied that *other* tradition.''

''I'm glad...'' Her eyes bright with desire, she drew up on tiptoe and kissed him, hugging his neck and pressing against him. ''Where's our bedroom, darling?''

Hunger, powerful and white-hot, coursed through him, the communication of her body wanton, even in its innocence. ''I thought you'd never ask,'' he murmured, surprised by the huskiness in his voice.

Lifting her in his arms, he whisked her back to the entry hall, and up the darkened stairs.

Josh felt good this morning. Not just physically sated—which he was. But good. He'd awakened late, around nine, to find Wendy sleeping beside him. She looked almost too tempting not to touch, with her hair tousled across her pillow, her body sleek and nude beneath the sheet, her lips pursed slightly as though in invitation. It seemed criminal to slide from the bed without another small taste.

But he knew one taste would lead to another and another, and very soon...

He shook the provocative vision from his brain as he quickly pulled on a pair of jeans, padding out of the bedroom and down the stairs. He wasn't a sex maniac, for Pete's sake. He could control himself. After all, Wendy was new to all this, and she would be a little uncomfortable today. He needed to give her time to become accustomed to the more intimate aspects of married life.

At the bottom of the stairs he spied Al's covered cage and decided to take the crow into the kitchen with him. He could use some company.

Once he had the coffee going and bacon frying, he went to the refrigerator and took out a carton of eggs. Turning he noticed Al, perched on the back of a chair. "Does she like her eggs scrambled or fried?" he asked.

The crow cocked her head and winked one pink eye. "Pretty boy, *kiss me!*"

He grinned. "'Fraid I'm a little tired, old girl."

He ambled to the range and set down the carton. "Scrambled," he said aloud. "I'm pretty good at that."

"You're pretty good at a lot of things."

Josh turned at the sound of Wendy's voice. She stood in the pantry entrance, leaning against the doorjamb. He looked her up and down, and grinned. She wore his polo shirt. Its four buttons were undone, showing off a nice glimpse of soft, pale flesh. She wore nothing else but his beige cotton socks, squished down around her ankles. No wonder he hadn't heard her.

"Hi." He turned his back on the stove and took her in. She was damned cute in his cast-off clothing, her hair mussed and her gaze drowsy from sleep. "I was about to scramble eggs. Is that okay with you?"

She pushed away from the wall and began to walk toward him, her approach soundless and surprisingly sexy. Though his shirt hem hit her at mid-thigh, he didn't think he'd ever seen any sight quite so erotic. Those slender, well-proportioned legs were smooth and pale, yet subtle muscle flexed beneath her skin, reminding him of how those legs had clasped him to her last night, so possessively, so passionately.

Heat rushed through him, warming his blood and clenching his gut. When she reached him, she slid her arms around him and kissed his chest. ''I want you for breakfast,'' she murmured, her lips tickling his bare skin.

He chuckled at her fetching wantonness. *Oh, Lord, keep me focused,* he pleaded inwardly, trying to maintain control. ''We need to eat,'' he said. ''To keep up our strength.''

''*Cash!* No checks!'' Al squawked.

Wendy laughed, lifting her face to look into her new husband's eyes. ''Al's a romantic fool.''

Josh grinned, hugging her. ''She propositioned me before you came in.''

''Oh?'' Wendy's eyebrows rose playfully. ''And what did you do?''

''I told her I was tired.''

Her cheeks flushed prettily and he would have bet anything she was thinking about the explosive abandon of their lovemaking. Stepping back from him she took his hand. ''Tired, hmmm?'' Leading him to the small kitchen table, she pulled out the chair nearest the window and across from Al. ''You sit. I'll scramble the eggs.''

''I don't mind,'' he said, but she nudged his hip with hers. ''Sit. I'll bring you coffee.''

He obliged, enjoying the sight as she filled a mug, returning with it and a brief kiss on his cheek.

He sipped and relaxed, watching her as she cracked eggs and scrambled them over the butane flame. The coffee was good, if he did say so himself. The kitchen smelled great. He inhaled, lounging back. The air had been nippy when he'd gotten up, but with the stove going and the sun shining in the window, it was nice in here.

Watching Wendy was nice, too. He was a little surprised at how much he enjoyed this. He didn't know what he'd expected to feel the first morning after his wedding. Sexually satisfied, he supposed. And he did—but not like all the other mornings with other women, when he'd left without breakfast, looking forward to escaping to his office.

His glance trailed over Wendy as she stirred the eggs. The beige polo shirt had slipped off one pale shoulder, and he experienced a strong urge to kiss the flesh revealed there. It was odd, he mused, but he felt strangely contented this morning. It was almost like coming home after a long, dreary trip.

She turned around, returning his smile. "Toast?"

He picked up his orange juice glass. "To you."

She laughed, a tinkling sound that warmed his belly. "Thank you, kind sir." She curtsied. "Let me rephrase. Would you like some toast with your eggs?"

"Oh," he teased. "I'm game if you are."

"Wild man," she kidded.

As she busied herself at the toaster, Josh laced his fingers behind his head and observed her. The way she separated slices of bread and then stuck them into the four-slice mechanism gave him a rush. Making toast had never seemed like a sexually explicit activity before, but the way she did it was making him hot.

She went back to stir the eggs, then turned off the burner. "More coffee?" she asked.

"No, thanks." He inclined his head in a silent request that she join him.

"But the toast."

He grinned. "I need a kiss."

Her cheeks went all peachy. Lord, he loved that.

She padded over to him complaisantly, then startled

him when she straddled his lap and draped her arms loosely about his neck. ''You need a kiss, hmmm?''

He closed his eyes, collecting himself. Unfortunately, his strangled groan of desire made itself known. When he peered at her, she was watching him with eyes that seemed a lot more knowing than they had twenty-four hours ago. And they were twinkling. Yes, his bride had learned a few things about men recently. ''Is a kiss *all* you want, Mr. Raven?''

He swallowed, she was making it rough for him to keep his vow to take things slowly with her.

She smiled slyly. ''There's something else, isn't there?'' She didn't wait for him to respond. Her lips touched his, whisper-light at first, her arms curling tightly around him. Then suddenly her kiss became urgent, hungry.

He crushed her to him, his body growing aroused, his control and his interest in breakfast fading fast. He wondered if she was ready for the lesson about making love on the kitchen table, and was about to fling her on her back, when she ended the kiss, with a giggle. Her eyes were alight with feminine wiles. ''I thought so,'' she said.

She slid off him, and he could only stare as she walked calmly away. How could she do that when he felt like he'd touched a live wire and his body buzzed and sputtered from the shock. What in the hell was she doing? ''Where…'' It came out sounding like a rusty gate. He cleared his throat. ''Where are you going?''

She didn't respond until she'd opened the refrigerator and retrieved something. When she turned, her face held a triumphant grin. ''I bet you want some of this on your toast,'' she said softly, almost tauntingly, as she displayed a jar of gooseberry jam. *Hellfire! She'd certainly learned a thing or two about driving a man crazy.* Had he been that good a teacher, or did she have the tiniest little sadistic streak in her?

He sat forward, his second choice to doubling over in frustrated lust. But he was a man after all, and men didn't roll to the floor moaning in front of women if they could help it. "I don't want gooseberry jam," he said as evenly as he could.

With a loud "pop," the toaster sprang to life, displaying four pieces of toasted bread. "No jam?" Wendy asked, the twinkle in her eyes never brighter. "Well, then, I can't imagine what you might possibly want."

He rested his elbows on the table and gave her a you're-gonna-get-it smirk. Crooking a finger at her, he growled softly, "Come here, Mrs. Raven."

Her look of confusion had no more validity than a six dollar bill. "But the eggs are ready and so is the toast."

"To hell with 'em."

She set the jam on the counter, then eyed him coyly. "But, Josh, didn't you say we needed to eat to keep up our strength?" Crossing her arms before her, she went on. "And didn't you say you were tired?"

Her prim act was amusing, but he was in pain. His lips quirked, in spite of himself. "Do you write down *everything* I say?" He sat back. "Come over here."

She grinned, and with a saucy turn, disobeyed him. "I'll get the toast."

"You're gonna *be* toast if you don't get over here, wife."

She stopped in the act of reaching for the first piece. "Oh?" Pointedly turning her back on him, she went on with her toast gathering. "Joshua Raven, I'd hate to think you're trying to boss me around."

"Young lady, if I could get up from this chair, I'd—I'd...."

She twisted back. "Fall to the floor into a writhing wad of seething lust?" Her lips quirked impishly.

"That's not funny—*correct* but not funny!" Josh shook his head at her, fighting a grin. "You know what you've done to me, you vixen."

She shoved a strand of hair behind her ear, her expression earnest. "I've done no more to you than you did to me weeks ago, with only a smile."

Her soft admission did something strange to his insides. He grew serious and sat back, feeling less playful. *Lord, she loved him.* He'd allowed himself to forget that, as he'd selfishly reveled in their shared gratification. Last night she'd shown him how much she cared, giving herself freely, taking his coaching on how to please and how to receive pleasure. She'd done things to him—with him—earthy, brazen things that had been, on her part at least, pure, unselfish devotion.

His old pal Guilt swooped down to peck at his eyes. With a grin he hoped didn't look too rueful, he murmured, "On second thought, maybe we'd better eat." He pushed up to stand, stifling a groan as he forced his body to straighten. "I'll serve the eggs. You butter the toast."

When he brushed past her, she hugged his waist. "Are you okay?"

He kissed the top of her head. "I'm fine."

"Did I do something wrong?"

His chuckle was dark and ironic. "No, Wendy. Don't even think that." With his hands on her upper arms, he pressed her away. "We shouldn't waste the food, that's all."

"It wouldn't go to waste." She looked perplexed and disappointed. "Al would eat it."

He smiled down at her. "Al's already too fat."

The bird squawked on cue, and Josh was glad to see Wendy's lips curl upward.

"We'll eat, then we'll—think of something else to do." Unable to help himself, he kissed her rosy cheek.

"But won't we get stomach cramps?"

He burst out laughing. Slinging an arm around her, he scooped up the skillet and carried it to the table. "Maybe. But just between us, I'm not planning to make love to you in the lake this morning. So I don't think we'll drown."

"Oh..." He could feel her self-deprecating laughter in their close contact.

Five minutes later, with sun shining in the kitchen window, warming Josh's back, Wendy jumped up, toast in hand. "Oh, I forgot! I want to try that gooseberry jam." She scooped up the jar from the tile countertop and skimmed out a half teaspoonful, dumping it on what was left of her piece. "I gather it's one of your favorites, since it's here."

He eyed her with amusement, accepting the jar. He liked gooseberry jam, but he was in the mood for something much warmer and sweeter at the moment.

"Wow," Wendy said, chewing. "It's tangy." She glanced his way and Josh noticed her eyes were watering.

He spread some on his slice. "Tangy, huh? Is that a nice way of saying you hate it?"

She giggled, swallowing. "No, it's really pretty good."

More to indulge her than in any real interest in food,

he took a bite. "I don't insist you learn to love gooseberry jam just because you married me."

"I love it. And I love you." She smiled. "I'm so happy." Her tender expression sent a shaft of renewed desire through him.

"You know what I want to do, Josh?"

He had no clue, and shrugged. But he hoped she wanted to straddle him again so he could get on with his lesson about making love to her on the kitchen table. He set down his toast, just in case. "What?"

She stood, and his heart rate shot up. This was a good sign.

"I'm going to call Judy and tell her how wonderful her sauce is."

He looked at her in disbelief, experiencing a slight let-down. "You want to call your neighbor and talk about marshmallow mint sauce—on our honeymoon?"

She grinned at him, her expression impish. "Why not? Do you have urgent plans?"

"You bet I have urgent plans," he said, mock reproach in his tone. "You're trying to kill me, aren't you?"

She walked over to him and put his face between her hands, kissing him, her lips sweet and full of promises. "It's such a little thing and she'd be so thrilled."

When she drew away, he forced himself to sit back. Damn, why was he suddenly jealous of her fondness for a bashful, well-meaning neighbor? This was stupid. Wendy had an urge to do a nice thing. What was wrong with that? He counted to ten and smiled. "Fine. Good idea."

"I knew you'd agree. I'll tell her hello for you, too." She kissed her fingertips then brushed his cheek with them. "Where's the phone, sweetheart?"

"My briefcase in the entry hall."

"Your briefcase?" She cocked her head in question. "Don't tell me you plan to conduct *business* on our honeymoon."

Another stab of guilt made him wince inwardly. How did he explain to her that this honeymoon was business—that he hadn't foreseen enjoying her, being with her, wanting her...

He lifted a skeptical brow. "Who's making the calls?"

She laughed and blew him a kiss. "Finish your breakfast. I'll be right back."

He crossed his arms, looking as stern as he could. "Two minutes."

"One and a half." She turned away, then looked over her shoulder. "Guess what I'm thinking."

He grinned. "You can't remember Judy's phone number?"

She laughed. "No, silly, I love you."

She was suddenly and silently gone. His gaze remained trained on the pantry door for a full minute. Finally, he shook his head. "I haven't guessed right once." Facing Al across the table, he grinned at the bird. "She's pretty cute."

Al flapped her wings. "Roll me over in the clover!" she shrieked, sidestepping along the chair left and then right. *"Kiss me!"*

Josh picked up his fork. "Not a chance, kid. I'm hot for your mom."

Intent on proving to himself—and to his playful, seductive bride—that he was a man of boundless control, a man who couldn't be twisted around a comely finger—he finished his bacon and ate a couple of bites of toast and jam.

Attempting to take his mind off his need to charge after her and christen the entry hall with reckless lovemaking, Josh watched Al do a perky little side-to-side dance on the chair edge. He chuckled as the bird wriggled her tail feathers in what looked like a blatant come-on. ''You're bad, Alberta.''

''Bad to the bone!'' she chirped, executing another thoroughly bawdy wiggle.

Josh roared with mirth, curiously contented, in light of his situation. Honeymoons—even with clowning crows—were damn nice, he decided. Wendy was better than nice. He had a feeling these next two weeks were going to be more rewarding than he'd imagined—and in ways that had nothing to do with his corporate bottom line.

Something warm and wet splattered his chest. At the same time he heard a loud clank. His glance shot to his plate where he noticed a swath had been cut through the middle of his meal. Globs of egg were scattered across the table and all up and down his belly and chest.

Another crash, this one louder, drew his gaze to the far kitchen wall. A small dark chunk of plastic lay on the floor amid yellow bits of egg. He looked closer, realizing the mangled casualty had once been his cell phone.

''What the hell...'' Jerking around, he saw Wendy framed in the pantry door. Her body was rigid and she looked—

''You—you *snake!*'' she hissed.

CHAPTER SEVEN

JOSH grew wary. Something was very wrong with Wendy. He'd never seen her angry, but if he didn't miss his guess, she was homicidal. Her features were hard as her gaze bored into his. She looked like she planned to draw blood.

In her hand she held—or rather wadded—a sheet of paper. "Wendy—honey?" he asked softly, cautiously. "Is something wrong?"

With his quiet question, her body stiffened further, her gaze flinging bolts of killer lightning. "Don't *honey* me, you belly-crawling *weasel!*" she shot in a curt, explosive salvo. "You mud-wallowing *pig!* You—you lying *bastard!*"

She flung the crumpled document at him, smacking him squarely in the center of his chest. "I never want to see you again—as long as I live!" The last came out splintered and broken. As she spun away, Josh heard a strangled sob.

In a confused trance, he took a step to follow her, to ask what had happened to make her so furious. But an instant later, his brain caught on the fact that the mangled page at his feet might hold his answer. He bent to retrieve it. Standing, he smoothed out the sheet. It startled him to notice the page held Gower Isaac's familiar, silver letterhead. Beneath it, a short note was scrawled in Gower's hand.

Josh frowned, perplexed. He'd never seen this letter before. Had Gower slipped it into his briefcase sometime after the wedding, yesterday? Why? He scanned the message. *Josh, my boy, you've held up your part of our bargain by marrying my daughter. Now, I'll do mine. The stock transfer will be complete by the time you return from your honeymoon. Congratulations. I don't have to tell you that you've made yourself a good deal.*

A good deal!

Josh experienced a rush of murderous rage. How could Gower have done such a thing—when it had been Gower, himself, who'd made Josh swear Wendy must never know she was part of the merger?

He sucked in a breath, then blew it out between clenched teeth. Fury coursed through him and his body began to shake with it. "Damn the man to a bottomless pit in hell for this!" His glance snapped toward the empty door where Wendy had stood a moment before. He recalled the sound of her sob, the tortured look of betrayal in her eyes, and felt sick. *Lord, what was he going to do? How was he going to fix this?* A hot wave of blood rushed up his neck and his world turned crimson. "*Damn* you, Gower," he thundered. "What have you done—what have *we* done—to your daughter?"

He heard a crash, and it brought him back to the here and now. She'd said she never wanted to see him again. What did she mean? With a stab of fear, he sprinted out of the kitchen. He reached the bottom of the staircase, but had to jump back to dodge the bouncing approach of her suitcase. "What the..." When it landed, he leaped over it and started up the stairs. "Wendy? Let me explain."

She stalked into his line of sight, looking as though she'd dressed hurriedly. She wore jeans, a pink T-shirt and sandals. Her hair was every bit as tousled as when she'd gotten up. She looked like a kitten—a furious kitten. "What's to explain?" she shot. "You made a great *deal!*"

The accusation was like a fist in his gut.

"Listen to me," he pleaded, taking the stairs two at a time. "Please—I didn't mean for you ever to know—"

"Don't you come near me, you—you—"

"I don't blame you for what you think of me," he broke in, wanting to pull her into his arms, soothe her misery, wipe away the hurt he'd done. "I know what I am, Wendy. I'm so sorry."

Her gaze shimmered and sparked, a dazzling mix of loathing and heartache. He reached for her, but she ducked, avoiding him. "Don't touch me!" She vaulted down the stairs. "I'm leaving you!"

"How?" he called, his voice tight and troubled. "We're in the middle of nowhere."

She stilled, turned, her face a study of anguish. "I—I'll call somebody." With the heel of her hand, she scrubbed away a tear. "I'll send for a boat."

She looked so stricken, so violated. So lost. Squeezing his eyes shut, he pinched the bridge of his nose, attempting to thwart a headache that had begun to pound between his ears. "We don't have a phone." He made himself look at her, to endure the spectacle of what he'd done. "Cell phones tend to disintegrate when used as torpedoes."

A flicker of realization dashed across her face. For a moment, her gaze grew bleak, but after a second her jaw hardened. "I'll get out of here. Mark my words, Mr. Raven..." Her voice rang with rebellion. "You can make all the dirty deals with my father you want. But I won't be a part of them." Whirling away, she grabbed her suitcase and wrenched open the door. "Put Alberta in her cage and bring her down to the dock for me."

The door slammed, echoing in Josh's brain, already hammered with guilt.

He grimaced. Shaking his head, he slumped against the banister. He was completely in the wrong, here, with no words to explain himself, no excuses she would ever accept. She'd been horribly deceived by her only living relative and her husband—the two people in the world she should have been able to trust. Opening his eyes, he peered at his chest, almost surprised he saw no gaping wounds. Her stare had fired off purple spikes of resentment so hostile, their stabs caused him physical pain.

Dammit, Raven, save the postmortem for later. Right now you have to stop your wife before she does something reckless and kills herself! With fresh resolve, he plunged down the staircase and out the front door. Off to his right, he caught movement and realized Wendy had dragged a canoe away from the side of the house. She'd made it to the sandy beach and was almost down to the water. "Wendy, stop!"

She looked up, her features cast in defiance. He winced at the fire he saw there. She said nothing, but went on with her work. With one huge tug, she dragged the canoe the rest of the way to the lake's edge. Hurrying around the craft, she pushed it halfway into the water. Josh headed toward her, running down the granite walkway. "Listen to me, Wendy. That damn thing will sink."

She had to have heard him, but she was making it clear she no longer gave a fig about anything that came out of his mouth. As she heaved the canoe into the water, she slid inside and grabbed the paddle.

"Wendy! It's got a hole in it!" Josh cried, padding barefoot to the water's edge. Stiff-backed, she settled in the bottom and paddled with all her might, out of his reach. The boat wobbled, and skewed slightly off to the right, but she got it under control. ''Wendy, don't be a fool!'' he pleaded gruffly.

Wendy had never been in a canoe before, but she'd seen the movie, *The Last of the Mohicans.* She knew you paddled on one side and then the other. Shifting to her knees, she leaned against the canoe's center thwart. The fact that she had no idea which way she should be going put a crimp in her escape plan, but she figured she would run into somebody—another house along the shoreline, a boat. *Something!*

She paddled, ignoring Josh's shouts. How dare he tell her there was a hole in the boat. There was no hole. She gritted her teeth and took another hard swipe with her paddle. Josh was a liar through and—through. She faltered, looking down. A little water sloshed around in the bottom. She hadn't noticed it before. She frowned, but discounted it. No doubt it had been there all the time, it just hadn't lapped against her knees until now.

She paddled furiously. Unable to help herself she glanced over her shoulder and was horrified to discover she had paddled and paddled and was only a stone's throw from shore. Josh wasn't where he had been the last time she looked. She scanned the shoreline, appalled to see her suitcase sitting on the dock where she'd set it before spying the canoe. Darn! The sight of Josh racing toward her had unsettled her so she'd forgotten all about it in her mad dash to escape.

Noticing movement, she shifted to spot her conniving husband, standing at the end of the pier. He was only about two canoe lengths from her. She wished she had a stone right now! Or a brick, or an African blow pipe. He made a big stationary target, standing there, his legs braced, his fists planted on trim hips, looking far from happy. "Dammit, Wendy, turn around while you still have time."

She stared at him—at his tall, lean good looks. Her heart fluttered with unruly disregard for the slime he was. Spinning away, she paddled like a crazed woman. When her small craft tottered in her efforts, water lapped further up her jeans. In the kneeling position, the lower half of her legs were definitely wet, now.

Her stomach lurched and she cast a worried glimpse down. A couple of inches of water had accumulated. *Oh, no! There is a leak, after all.* Josh hadn't been lying about this. Probably the first true statement he'd made since they'd met, the bum! She bit down hard on her lower lip and vacillated, halting her frantic paddling. Did she really want to be further out in the lake when the canoe sank?

"*Wendy!*" came Josh's gruff call. "Jump out and swim toward me."

She shifted. He was holding a life preserver tied to a rope. She didn't know where he'd come up with that. Apparently he could conjure life-saving equipment out of thin air. She swallowed hard around the lump in her throat, trying to hold back another sob. Too bad he couldn't conjure up a way to talk her out of hating his guts.

He'd made such beautiful love to her last night. Tears welled as she recalled how very, very believable his lovemaking had been. She'd never experienced anything so wondrous. She didn't even know such intimate bliss could exist between a man and a woman. A tear escaped, and she angrily wiped it away. Why did Joshua have to be such a lying rat? She'd been so happy only an hour ago, thinking she had what every woman dreamed of. And now—she had nothing.

"Wendy!" Josh called again, lifting the life preserver, perhaps thinking she hadn't noticed it. "Jump. I promise I'll get you."

The canoe was at a standstill, sluggish and riding low in the water. When she moved and the boat wobbled, the rolling water made her have to struggle to remain upright. She could feel her backside taking the first cold pats of the encroaching lake. In a moment she'd be swimming whether she jumped or not.

She'd be darned if she would go anywhere near Josh and his life preserver. She was a strong swimmer and making the beach from there was a piece of cake. Pushing up to stand, she faced the shore and dived. As she plunged into the murky depths, she become aware that the water not far under the surface was very cold—liquid ice. The shock of such stunning coldness made her expel the air in her lungs, and she paddled to the surface where the temperature wasn't quite so body-numbing. As she swam, her sandals fell away, but there was nothing to do about it. The lake was too frigid for lingering in search of discount store shoes.

Pumping her arms and kicking hard, she aimed for shore. Every so often she caught sight of Josh. Darn the man. He'd realized she wasn't heading toward him, so he loped back along the dock and leaped to the beach. With a sinking feeling, she knew she would have no choice but meet him when she made shore.

When her foot smacked sandy lake bottom, she shoved up to stand. Soaked to the skin and teeth chattering, she walked out of the lake as proudly as she could.

When Josh waded out to take her hand she jerked

from his touch and took a mighty swing at his jaw. Unfortunately, she missed, and the force she put into her attempt to knock him flat ended up tipping her off balance. She sprawled headfirst back into the water.

Sputtering, she propelled herself up to stand, batting sopping hair from her eyes. Still blinded by water, she heard him mutter a low oath. An instant later, she found herself in his arms, being lifted into the air. ''You—let me go!'' She wriggled and kicked, pushing against him. *''I hate you!''*

''Quit fighting me, Wendy. You'll have pneumonia if you don't get out of those wet things.''

''Good,'' she retorted, ''I want pneumonia!'' Her voice broke, and a bone-rattling shudder forced a delay in her struggle to get free.

''No, you don't,'' Josh said, more softly. ''You need your strength to murder me.''

She eyed him with scathing animosity. ''You think that's *not* my major goal?''

''I'm sure it is,'' he said, his expression bleak. ''I don't blame you.''

Wendy felt like she was breaking open, spilling pieces of herself—her heart, her mind, her soul—into a ruthless, chaotic wind. She doubted she could ever be whole again after what Josh had done. Her body quaked, her teeth banged against each other so hard she feared they would crumble. Tears flowed as though a dam had burst inside her heart.

Impotent from loss and sadness, and too cold to resist, she went limp in his arms. But the worst thing of all was how much it hurt to realize something inside still craved him, still loved him. With effort she battled down a stupid urge to cling to him, to beg him to love her back.

How could she have been so wrong about him? He was a man so devoid of feelings that he could manipulate her into making her fall in love with him. At least her mother had had the option of going into her business marriage with her eyes open.

It was all so horribly clear, now. Joshua Raven had used his abundant charisma to pull her into his trap, and being the naive fool that she was, she'd followed willingly. He must have found it hilarious to discover how easily she succumbed to his line of bull.

And her father. How could he have done this to her? His had been the first betrayal, but Josh had gone along willingly, uncaring, his blind greed dictating his every calculated move.

Well, Wendy Isaac Raven—she felt a stab at the realization that she shared his name—would *not* be Joshua Raven's possession, to shrivel and die the way her mother had. A cry of anguish tore from her throat, and her fight came back with a fury. She rammed an elbow in Josh's chest and was rewarded with a grunt of pain. She would not allow herself to be used this way. "Get your hands off me, Mr. Raven!"

She was surprised when he lowered her to her feet. Doubly surprised to discover she was back in the upstairs bedroom. "Strip, Wendy."

Her gaze flew to his. "G—get out-t-t of here!" Her teeth chattered so badly she could barely get the words out.

"Hell." He grabbed the hem of her shirt and yanked it up. "You're taking that thing off, *now.*"

She gasped as he forced the wet T-shirt over her head. When he tossed it aside, she instinctively covered her breasts. "What do you think..."

"Now the jeans."

He took hold of the waist snap and yanked it open. When he reached for the zipper, she slapped his hand away. "You have no right to touch me!"

Jaw working, he peered at her, his eyes dark, determined. "I'm your husband. I've touched you much more intimately than this." Brushing away her restraining fingers, he yanked the zipper tab down. Grabbing the jeans, he tugged. "Step out."

She'd dressed so hurriedly, she wore no underwear. Mortified, she attempted to hide herself, but it was impossible to screen everything his ungentlemanly behavior exposed. "I won't!" She stooped to reach for her jeans.

Before she could make good on her attempt, Josh swung her into his arms, one hand jerking the soggy denim off her feet. "While you soak in a hot bath, I'll start a fire." Wendy found herself settled into an empty bathtub. She scrambled to her knees, but he grasped her shoulder, pressing her down. "I'm not getting in, if that's what you're worried about. Sit still."

His rugged features were closed in firm resolve. His dark eyes dared her to disobey, very clearly communicating she was no match for his strength—if he chose to use it.

His macho tactics on the heels of his treachery, skewered her heart. But she knew brute strength would win out in the long run, and decided to save her energy for when she could better use it. "If you leave me alone," she retorted, grimly. "I'll take the bath."

His expression altered slightly, from resolute to dubious. "There's nowhere for you to go, Wendy. Outside that window is a long drop. Don't be a fool and try anything crazy, again."

Gritting her teeth, she dropped her gaze.

She heard movement, then the sound of water pouring from the tap. Warm and rejuvenating, it streamed across her frigid toes. "Promise?" he demanded, over the gurgling sound.

She closed her eyes, hating the fact that he was lounging on the edge of the tub, staring at her trembling nudity. This thuggish attitude toward her was no doubt his true one. He spoke no soft words, whispered no sweet lies about her loveliness, made no move to brush his fingertips or his lips along sensitive, secret places. She swallowed hard, working on building a healthy hatred worthy of such an egotistical lowlife. He was a morally corrupt beast, allowing her a glimpse of paradise, then snatching it away.

She bit back stinging accusations she wanted to spew at him. Instead, she nodded submissively. She was too mentally and emotionally exhausted to even dredge up the fortitude to look at him. At this moment, she needed sanctuary from his towering, unfeeling presence more than she needed retribution. *But that would come!*

Drawing herself into a protective ball, she covered her face with her hands. "Just go."

A snake. That's what Josh felt like as he stacked wood in the bedroom fireplace. A slithering viper. Ironically, he'd begun to feel less like one only this morning, when he'd awakened next to Wendy. She'd been lovely in the morning light, her lips parted in vague, oblivious invitation. He'd smoothed a strand of hair from her face, and almost given in to the urge to kiss the spot where the tendril had grazed her cheek. He'd felt almost whole, clean, lying there next to her. But now he felt like he'd been drilled in the belly with a load of buckshot.

Needing to keep busy, he got the fire going, and

spread her wet jeans and T-shirt on the stones of the outer hearth. He stilled, staring down at the pink shirt, recalling how the sight of Wendy rising from the lake had affected him. Soaked, the cotton knit plastered to her body, brazenly displayed the outline of her breasts. He'd found himself frozen—gaping. A rush of raw lust came to life in his gut. The sight had incapacitated him, and he'd been incapable of defending himself when she'd taken a swing at his jaw. He was lucky she'd missed.

Dragging a hand through his hair, he pulled his gaze from the T-shirt. "Raven, get a grip." Satisfying his lust was not on Wendy's agenda. Homicide was. For the sake of his mental health he'd better keep her out of wet T-shirts for the duration. And, for his physical well-being, he'd be smart to hide all sharp objects. It was crystal-clear his new wife despised him. Fury and pain sparked in her gaze like volcanic eruptions. He closed his eyes, releasing a store of pent-up and confused emotions in a drawn-out sigh.

He heard the bathroom door click, and glanced around. When his gaze locked with Wendy's, he detected an urge to retreat flicker in her gaze, but a second later, with the lift of her chin, it disappeared. "I—I need my clothes." She didn't quite meet his eyes.

He scanned her. She wore his oversize terry robe that had been hanging on a hook in the bathroom. Her hair was wet and slicked back. Her eyes were red and puffy. She looked so small, so fragile. So tragic. He experienced a jolt of self-disgust, a sensation that was beginning to feel all too common these days. With a nod, he left the room to fetch her things from the dock.

Bounding back up the stairs with her suitcase, Josh decided Wendy was going to hear his side whether she wanted to or not. It wasn't as black as she thought. After all, he'd married her honorably, hadn't he? Slinging open the door, he caught sight of her, huddled in the rocker facing the fire. Her feet were tucked beneath her. His white robe enveloped her completely to the tips of her fingers.

Only her dipped head was visible in all that soft terry. When he closed the door, she didn't seem to register his presence. That worried him. She hadn't gone into some sort of shock, had she? There wasn't any post-traumatic syndrome for finding out your husband lied about loving you, was there? He felt nausea churn his belly. "Look, Wendy," he began gently. "In this world, people sometimes marry for reasons more pragmatic than notions of infatuation. Lots of these couples stay married. My parents didn't marry for love, and they were happy."

Slowly she lifted her head and peered at him. Her glance ripped through him like talons. A heartbeat later she turned away. He felt the slash of her rejection, but forged on. "I want our marriage to work. I plan to be good to you." He lifted his hands in a beseeching gesture, though she wasn't looking in his direction. "I stopped seeing other women. That should prove I mean to be honorable."

She stared into the crackling fire. After a tension-filled minute, she looked at him. "How big of you." A tear materialized, trembled for an instant, then skimmed down her cheek. "Then again, what are a few sexual rendezvous more or less, compared to a multimillion-dollar business deal?" Turning away, she whispered tartly. "I *loathe* you, Joshua Raven."

The tone in her voice caused a heavy dullness to constrict his chest. He couldn't allow himself to accept that. Setting down her suitcase, he strode to stand before her.

Kneeling, he slipped a hand into her robe sleeve to take her fingers. "Wendy, I care for you. I really do."

Her recoil bordered on violence as she wrenched from his grasp. "I don't want to hear any more of your lies." She jumped up, scurrying to place the rocking chair between them. The robe sagged wide, displaying pale, soft flesh. She yanked the lapels together and marched further out of reach. "I've decided I'm going to camp out for the duration of the two weeks. Bird-watch."

He stood, frowning at this new twist. "Do *what?*"

She cast a savage glance his way. "I saw a sleeping bag in the closet and some binoculars in the dresser. *I'm going to bird-watch!*" she repeated, slowly and distinctly, as though gritting it out through clenched jaws would frighten him away from disagreeing with her.

Fat chance! He took a step toward her, but with her shuffling retreat to the far side of their bed, he gave it up. She was having nothing to do with him, so he might as well face it. "Have you ever camped out in your life?" he asked, trying to be the voice of reason.

"That's none of your business."

"But, Wendy—"

"Get out of here and let me dress. If I can't leave you by water, I'm going to at least put some acreage between us."

"There are wild animals out there," he coaxed. "Bears. Even a moose in a bad mood could kill you."

Uncertainty skittered across her features, and Josh felt a surge of progress. "What if you get lost?" he pressed. "You can't eat off the land. You're a city girl."

She swallowed visibly, opened her mouth to speak, but no words came. He almost smiled. Success! Victory! He decided to add icing to the cake of her growing misgivings. "Not to mention poisonous snakes."

"Snakes?" she spat. Cinching the robe's belt tighter, as though the word had struck a painful cord, she scowled at him. "There can't be any snakes out there that are more dangerous than the one in here!"

He flinched at her harshness. "I never meant to hurt you, Wendy," he murmured, meaning it. "Honestly."

Her lips trembled and her eyes brew bright with new tears. "I'm going." Her stance unyielding, her teary glare damned him to hell. "I'd rather be eaten by a bear than share this house with you."

He was so frustrated he wanted to bash the stick-work rocker against the wall and turn it into high-priced kindling. Clenching his jaw and his fists, he battled to hold his temper. "You're my wife, and you're *staying.*"

Lifting a stubborn chin, her eyes shot defiant sparks.

CHAPTER EIGHT

THE first day Josh ever saw Wendy he'd sensed she was the type to act on her feelings—a "Go for it!" kind of woman. For once, he was sorry he was right.

Wendy had made it excruciatingly clear she had no intention of breathing the same slime-polluted air he breathed. She would not be deterred in her crazy scheme to camp out in the woods. His only alternative, short of binding and gagging her, was to let her go. The binding and gagging idea held merit—especially since he knew she'd be in less danger that way. Unfortunately, in her current mood, he had a sinking feeling she would simply gnaw through the ropes and escape.

He managed to get her to compromise, thank heaven. She would make camp on a rise within sight of the house. That way, if there was trouble she could run to safety. Not to mention that food and logs for her campfire were nearby.

He exhaled, worried. She wasn't exactly Dr. Livingstone. *And why should she be?* he chided inwardly. She hadn't intended to get her Girl Scout camping badge on this trip. She'd expected to share a romantic honeymoon hideaway with her husband.

Josh trekked up the wooded incline a few paces ahead of Wendy, leading her to her campsite. This had been another hard-fought compromise, being allowed to show her the way. His wife wasn't much in the mood for negotiating. Getting this far with her had been as formidable a task as any business transaction he'd ever won in a boardroom. He didn't dare presume it was a step forward, but if he set up camp, himself, at least he could make sure she didn't wander too far astray.

The late morning air was brisk and thick with the clean scent of pine. Not far off the trail, an effervescent waterfall flowed over a granite shelf. Sparkling even in shadow, it collected in a crystal-clear pool of smooth, gray rock below. Josh breathed deeply of the pristine woods and found himself experiencing an unexpected burst of optimism. How could the beauty and calm of this vast, uninterrupted wilderness not assuage Wendy's bruised heart? Maybe a little time exposed to the idyllic splendor of the Adirondacks wasn't a bad idea.

He checked over his shoulder to see how she was keeping up. Their glances clashed for an instant before she turned pointedly away. She carried the bedroll she'd found; the binoculars dangled around her neck—as though she had the faintest idea what to do with them. He'd bet his last dollar that Alberta was the only bird she'd ever watched in her life.

The white crow clung to Wendy's head, visibly distressed at being dragged out into the wilds. Wendy had been stubborn about that, too. She wanted Alberta with her. What exactly did she think he planned to do to her precious crow—eat it?

The path he led her over was moss-covered, and had a pleasant texture—solid, yet spongy—a living carpet. When he reached the crest of the rise, he dropped an armload of firewood and his shovel. He settled the basket of food he'd brought on a large rock. Straightening, he scanned the clearing. This was nice, just as he remembered. Through the trees to his left he could see a rocky ledge overlooking the lake. At least nothing could attack her from that side.

The clearing was about the size of an average bedroom, with a dense growth of pines, maples and birch trees serving as the bower's woodland walls.

He heard Wendy enter the clearing and turned. With a nod, he indicated the center of the campsite. "I'll build your fire there."

She dropped the bedroll. "Don't bother. I can do it." She sounded vaguely breathless from the steep trek.

"Sure you can, Dan'l Boone," he muttered cynically. Grabbing his shovel, he went about clearing away dead leaves and pine needles. "This is a bad idea, Wendy." He eyed her as she unrolled her bed.

"You're a fine one to talk about bad ideas!" With an accusing stare, she lowered herself to sit. Alberta fluttered and squawked, attempting to maintain purchase on Wendy's head. "Go back to the house. I can make my own fire."

He tossed aside the shovel and retrieved some firewood. "Once I get it started you can keep it going." He arranged the cut wood in the cleared area, using dry leaves as kindling. Once the fire was going good, he stood and peered at her. Neither she nor Al looked very relaxed. The sight roused a surge of helpless irritation. "Wendy, you don't even have a tent. This is crazy."

Her gaze brimmed with fire and pain. "I'll be fine," she countered, each word fired like a bullet.

Cold fingers of contrition tightened around his belly. Dammit, she wouldn't be fine! Why didn't she see that? *Lord, please don't let it be that she doesn't care what happens to her!* At his wit's end, he shook his head, trying for composure. "At least let me take Alberta back. She's scared stiff."

Wendy made a pained face, an indication Al's claws were yanking at her hair. "*Ouch!*" She lifted her hands to the bird's talons, attempting to loosen her grip. "Al, you're hurting me."

"Hide me!" Al screeched. *"Let's scram! It's the cops!"*

"She doesn't sound pleased," Josh prompted. He held out a hand. "Come here, Alberta, honey. We'll go back and have a Twinkie."

Al flapped her wings and crowed. "*Kiss me,* pretty boy." Two seconds later she lit on Josh's head. *"Let's scram! Caw—caw!"*

Josh surveyed Wendy with compassion. She was hunched on the bedroll, her arms hugging her knees. Her posture spoke eloquently of her anxiety. "It's best if Al stays inside. Deep down, you know that." Crossing his arms before him, he exhaled tiredly. "Would it do me any good to tell you again that you're better off in the house, too?"

She shifted to her knees and crossed her arms over her binoculars, mirroring his disapproving stance. *Blast it,* she was one stubborn woman!

"Just take my crow and go," she bit out, sounding as obstinate as ever. Yet, a new, forlorn note tinged her words. Josh sensed she felt she'd been betrayed by everyone and everything she cared about—and now even her pet had deserted her.

Facing away, she fumbled for the field glasses and put them to her eyes. Josh glanced in the direction she'd turned, and frowned, suspecting the abrupt move was an effort to disguise a new bout of crying. Whatever else she intended by the move, there was no mistaking her dismissal.

"Okay, okay," he mumbled. "I can take a hint." He turned to go, then shifted back. This time he caught the flash of a tear on her cheek as it reflected firelight. Guilt assailed him and he bit back a curse. "If you need me, Wendy—I'll—just call out."

She didn't turn, didn't act as though she'd heard. She merely held that stupid pair of binoculars to her eyes. Another tear blazed with reflected firelight. The sight put a mean torque on the knife in his belly.

Clenching his jaws against the ache, he lurched out of the clearing and trudged toward the house.

Hours later the knife still twisted mercilessly as he hid in the shadows, watching Wendy cry. He had no intention of allowing her to stay out there all by herself, a naive city girl, weeping in the wilderness. She was so lost in her sorrows, a bear could have lumbered into her camp and had her half devoured before she'd even notice.

Only moments after depositing Alberta safely in her cage, Josh stealthily returned, clambering into a nearby spruce. His elevated perch gave him an overview of the area, just in case some wild, deadly animal roamed too close. He'd be damned if he would break Wendy's heart, then let physical harm come to her, too. He liked her—a lot.

His lips lifted in a sneer of self-loathing, and he muttered, "So, this is how you treat the people you like, Raven?" He scanned his wife, lying facedown on the bedroll, her face tucked into one elbow. Every so often, between the twitter of birds and the rustle of a breeze, he could detect her muffled sobs. "You're a fine man," he muttered. "I'm proud all to hell of you, buddy."

His mind drifted to last night, of her kisses, how her mouth had set fire to his blood, made him forget he wasn't in love with her. He'd thought of nothing but pleasing her, teaching her things she learned so willingly—so exquisitely.

He bit back a curse, snatching his mind from thoughts of Wendy's lips, Wendy's sweet, soft sighs, Wendy's yielding body and her unschooled, yet exhilarating touch. And those neon, angel eyes, glistening with an otherworldly light that stole his breath. He groaned, then snapped his glance back to focus on his wife. She didn't move, didn't react. She hadn't heard him. Good. Leaning back against the tree trunk, he clutched hard at the branch under his left arm. What was his problem? He wasn't a man disposed to drift off into daydreams.

A snap of a branch off to his right drew him up, alert. He craned around to see what made the sound, visions of a six-foot bear exploding in his brain. Quietly, he drew up his shotgun, prepared to shoot to kill if Wendy's safety was threatened.

Then he saw it, a doe, lapping from the brook. Close by her side, her fawn sniffed the air, then dipped its tawny head for a drink. Josh sank back, his body prickling with the rush of adrenaline. He inhaled deeply, grateful for this reprieve, at least. Closing his eyes, he lolled his head against the rough bark. "Lord..." He sucked in another breath, working to get his thudding heart under control. "Don't make me spend the next two weeks in a tree."

The wedding had been last Saturday. Today was Wednesday, or was it Thursday? Josh was so brain dead he was no longer sure. And he'd spent so much time in a tree he felt "Raven" was more than just his name. He was afraid he might get a sudden urge to fly south for the winter.

He chuckled, then clamped his jaws together. Running a hand across his eyes, he squinted in a futile attempt to clear his vision. He was too tired to be much good to

Wendy. He had to get some sleep. The short catnaps he'd taken when he went back to the house to bathe and eat, hadn't been enough. He was getting addled from fatigue, laughing out loud at his own twisted thought processes.

With a weary groan, he picked his way down the now familiar branches of the spruce. The night was pitch-black, low-ceilinged, silent and perfect for sleep. Jumping silently to the ground, he crept to the edge of the clearing. Wendy was curled in the sleeping bag, her back to him. The fire had dwindled to coals. Soundlessly, he made his way to the stack of wood and fed the ebbing campfire. A breeze swept through, chilling him through his wool shirt.

As the fire licked at the new logs, Josh observed Wendy's face. There was little peace in her expression. Even in sleep, her features were pinched and sad. The dull ache that seemed to have ridden his chest forever grew sharp and he ran both hands through his hair. "Oh, Wendy," he moaned. "What can I do?" The question came out in a melancholy whisper that vanished on a cold breeze before it could reach her ears—as ineffective as he felt.

Suddenly he didn't give a damn about anything. He was too exhausted to think. Besides, what good had all his thinking done him? He had a strong need to comfort her, even if it meant she would spit and kick and bite and defy the overture with all her strength. He was too tired to care what physical blows she might inflict on him. He was emotionally beaten, so what was a little blood and a few broken bones?

In two steps he was beside her, lowering himself to the ground. He was so tired he couldn't bother about the right or wrong of it, and pressed against her back. He encircled her protectively with one arm. "Good night, my little spitfire," he murmured into her hair. He inhaled her scent, then smiled at the gentle memories it conjured.

That was Josh's last thought until peachy fingers of dawn stretched into the glade, waking him.

It was weird how his spirits seemed lighter today, and it had nothing to do with sleep. It had been Wendy's nearness, he knew—and sheltering her in his embrace.

As he returned to the shadows, a rush of satisfaction completely out of proportion to the situation lightened his step.

Wendy stirred and rubbed her eyes. She didn't want to wake up. She'd been dreaming about Josh—about how it felt to be held in his arms, to be gathered close against his big, solid body. She'd known this feeling of belonging, of being cherished, for only one night, but the memory was so strong it almost seemed as though...

She forced herself to open her eyes. There was no sense dwelling on a foolish dream. Another day of misery and loneliness had begun, and she might as well get on with it. She realized now she'd done a stupid thing by insisting she camp out. She should have taken Josh up on his offer to sleep out here, yielding the house to her. At least, if he was the one camping out, she would have—what? A roof over her head to cry under? Yes—but it was *Josh's* roof. Everything in that house belonged to Josh. She didn't intend to become one of *Josh's* things. One of *his* purchases. In one of *his* houses.

Heaving a sigh, she clambered out of the bedroll. Her glance caught on the basket sitting nearby. It was different from the one that had been there when she'd gone to sleep. Her attention flicked to the bonfire, blazing away. That was impossible—unless. She pushed her hair off her face, reluctant to think of Josh so near, attempting to make amends in small ways.

She knew he was suffering, too. But his suffering had to do with being found out, not heartbreak. His suffering had to do with figuring out a way to get back into her good graces so he could keep his corporation. His suffering involved corporate survival, not emotional demise. She supposed, if she allowed herself to be objective, his suffering—considering what he truly *loved* in this world—was as acute as hers.

She bit down on her lip until it throbbed with her pulse. Pressing her hands to her face, she gulped down a whimper of despair. She had to get over this thing! Be strong! Joshua was only a man—and not a very nice man, at that. She must put this behind her and move on. She must grow whole again. It might take time, but she couldn't let the treachery of her father and one unscrupulous corporate shark get the better of her.

Imposing iron control over her emotions, she made herself reach for the basket. She was so sick at heart she wasn't hungry, but she had to eat—even if the breakfast was an offering from her two-faced husband. There was no sense in being any more childish about this mess than she'd already been.

She lifted the basket lid to spy a thermos. Coffee. That would taste awfully good. The morning air was nippy. And muffins. Oranges. She unscrewed the lid of the thermos, using it as her coffee mug. The steaming brew smelled strong and delicious. Sipping she munched on a bran muffin.

How sweet life could have been if she were only inside the house, sharing this breakfast with a man who loved her. Such seemingly small things were what made life a paradise on earth. Not fame or fortune. Just a good cup of coffee and a muffin, and the right man smiling at you from across the breakfast table.

A new rush of tears stung her eyes, but she choked them back. *She would not cry about him any longer.* She'd spent all the tears she ever wanted to spill over that—that shifty, diabolical con artist! She would bide her time. The first boat she saw that came close enough to the inlet that led into their secluded cove, she'd wave and make such a screaming racket, they'd have to come check on her.

Then there was the mail boat. You'd think somebody would write them a letter. One letter! Unfortunately the U.S. mail didn't seem to know they were there, since the mail boat hadn't come to check for outgoing posts. She had to hope somebody—*anybody*—would send them a letter. And soon.

Pushing up to stand, she took her breakfast to the ledge overlooking the inlet. These past four days, the peaceful view had helped fortify her battered soul. The unruffled water shone like sterling silver at this time of day. In the afternoons it turned a rich blue-green. Deep and calm and full of peace.

Across the water lay boundless forested hills. The lush terrain rose and fell, rose and fell, again and again and again, until the distance became so great their vivid hues dissolved and blurred.

Though immersed in great sadness, Wendy couldn't help but be touched by the grandeur of this protected, eastern wilderness. She sat simply staring for so long, time seemed to disappear. But the ache in her heart remained, her only constant in a world of deceit and ruined dreams.

She didn't see Josh all day. The time Wendy spent in the house, bathing, changing clothes and visiting Al, her senses were fine-tuned for the sound of a door opening. The whole place smelled of him, and she inhaled, taking his essence deep inside her. Imbecile that she was, she faced the hard truth that it wasn't only his scent she missed. Her heart seemed bent on craving his nearness, her eyes pined for a glimpse of his face. Even her arms ached to hold his head against her breast once more, her fingers caressing the silky bliss of his hair.

Where is he? her mind cried. He couldn't have left her all alone at his secluded home. There was no way out. Or did he know of a secret road? Had he hiked to some woodland hamlet where he was now on the phone, scheming with her father about ways to salvage their mutually profitable deal? Ways to get Wendy under control again? Or was he salving the wounds of this business setback in some convenient woman's arms? She felt a twinge with the picture that evoked. She hated feeling anything. She didn't want to be jealous. Why, oh, why did she have to be? She wanted to hate the man. He deserved her hatred.

Where was he? Okay, so she'd made it blisteringly clear she'd rather be devoured by wild beasts than see him again, but...*but she wanted to see him again, drat her witless hide!*

Deep in the night, Wendy was hunkered down in her bedroll. Though emotionally exhausted she slept fitfully. Finally, so tired she felt drugged, she managed to drift off. Somewhere in her dreamy reverie, she fastened onto the fact that she was no longer chilled. The fire crackled, shooting sparks toward heaven, while she lay there, secure within the haven of loving arms. *What a wonderful dream.*

The fire smelled nice. She inhaled. Along with wood smoke, she detected Josh's unmistakable scent. She smiled, sucking in another draft of fragrant air. Nobody smelled as nice as Josh. She drifted happily along in her private oblivion, willing the manifestation to stay, to comfort and complete her—if only for tonight.

Turning, she snuggled in the crook of her dream lover's arm. Her lips brushed the hollow of his throat and she impulsively kissed him, his pulse beat registering against her lips. Releasing a contented sigh, she slipped an arm about his waist, hugging him close. Her unruly behavior didn't trouble her. After all, you couldn't control your dreams, could you? Besides, when she woke up, she probably wouldn't remember any of it.

A pity.

His breath feathered her hair, warm and sweetened with his essence. His lips brushed her temple in a light kiss. Josh was such a gentle, caring man—in her dreams.

Wendy heard a hissing sound. Hissing?

Hiss. Hiss.

What was it? She frowned. No! She didn't want her dream to change. She didn't want a snake to be in her dream. Something cold hit her on the forehead. Then again, but this time the strange cold thing splatted on her cheek.

''Wendy, darling—it's raining.''

She fought this mutation in her fantasy. She didn't want snakes or rain right now. She wanted Josh! She wanted his kisses, his—

''Wendy, wake up,'' a deep, male voice whispered. ''It's raining.''

She fought encroaching consciousness, but her brain conspired against her. The fog began to lift and she squinted, rubbing her eyes. As she did, the back of her hand was smacked by a large, cold raindrop.

"We'd better go inside," the voice coaxed.

She stilled. Sliding her hand away from her eyes, she was startled to see a face looming above hers. *Josh's face?* Another gaggle of hisses caught her attention. Befuddled, she shifted to stare at the fire. Raindrops popped and sizzled as water met flame. Wood smoke rode heavy in the air, and she coughed. It *was* raining; that was real enough. But the part about Josh—that had been a dream.

Hadn't it?

Her groping mind cleared in a rush. She jerked around to assure herself that her dream had vanished, as it should have, or… Oh, dear! He hadn't been a dream. Josh was there. *Lying beside her.*

He pushed up on an elbow and gazed down at her. He wasn't smiling, but his eyes held such gentleness, she had to will her anger to rise up and shatter a surge of desire. Defensively, she pressed him away. "What are you doing here?"

"Sleeping."

"Sleeping?" She scrambled to sit, putting distance between them. "What does that mean—*sleeping?*"

He came up on one knee, taking her arm. "We'll talk about it inside. It's raining."

She tugged from his grasp. "I know it's raining! Now answer my question."

He stood. With the toe of his boot, he scattered burning logs, kicking dirt over the fire. "You get the basket." He plucked up the bedroll, shaking leaves and dirt from it. "The forecast calls for rain for the next several days. You have to come inside."

He flung the bedroll over one shoulder and took her arm. "Basket?" he reminded.

In an odd daze, she did as he softly commanded. Part

of her wanted to fight him, to plunk herself down in the rain, like a boulder, and stay until she grew moss. But the other part of her—the part that sang with the touch of his fingers on her arm, the part still tingling from the kiss on her temple, the part dizzy from his scent—*that* part kept her from shouting out denials and rejections.

That disobedient, perverse, moronic, lovesick part coerced her into putting one foot in front of the other, one foot in front of the other, shuffling after him, like a zombie, as he drew her toward the house.

Halfway back the rain got serious, and Wendy snapped out of her trance.

CHAPTER NINE

WENDY'S feline growl startled Josh. She wrenched from his grasp, the hasty move almost upending her on the mossy slope. When he made a grab for her arm, she slapped his hand away. "Oh, no, you don't!" She stumbled a step backward.

Soaked to the skin, her hair plastered around her crimson face, she wagged a finger at him. "You're not using your charm to hypnotize me back under your spell!"

Needles of rain pelted his head and shoulders. He lifted the bedroll like a hood, extending one end in her direction. "Get under here with me. This is no place to discuss it."

She eyed him with abhorrence. "I'm not slipping under any more covers with you, Joshua Raven!" She poked his chest. "Let me put it in a way a tough businessman like you can understand." She swiped rain from her eyes. Or were they tears? "That scheme you and Daddy cooked up—that marriage gimmick—it's a *deal-breaker,* buddy." She poked again. Hard. "Nothing—*nothing* you can do or say will ever change that. You might as well face that fact and deal with it!"

The repeated stabs of her finger caused him little physical pain. The pain came from the necessity of witnessing her sadness. She tried to mask it with anger, which was probably healthy. But he wasn't fooled.

He felt helpless, at a loss for what to do. He was a son of a bitch; he knew that. But he was a weary son of a bitch. He was weary from thinking about what he'd done and continually cursing himself. He'd been weary for days. And *yes,* he was angry, too. He was angry at Gower and angry at himself. And he was starting to get mad at Wendy. She was too pigheaded for her own good, standing there in the cold, dawn rain, shaking violently as her body fought the loss of heat.

Something in him snapped, allowing his fury, his helplessness, and his frustration to break free, take charge. He grabbed her poking hand and growled, "*Enough!*" An instant later, his rebellious wife was slung over his shoulder, her derrière wriggling next to his face. Casting a glance at her fidgety bottom as though in conversation with it, he shouted, "You're the most obstinate woman I've ever had the misfortune to marry!"

She slapped ineffectually at his backside. "Put me down, you *ape.*" With his arms wrapped around her legs, she was fairly well hobbled, but that didn't stop her from trying to kick and flail. "I've—*oof!*—never been manhandled in my life!"

"It's a first for me, too, sweetheart!" he yelled over the driving rain. "But if it makes you feel better, it looks like you're going to get carried over the threshold a second time."

She squirmed. "I won't! *Oof!* Not by you!"

"Who's going to stop me?"

She beat at his back with her fists. "Put me down. I'm going to throw up!"

He mounted the stone patio steps with a less jarring stride. Her ride over his shoulder wasn't the most comfortable mode of transportation in the world, and he didn't want to make her ill.

"I said, put me down!"

Walking to the door, he swung it wide and stepped

into the narrow foyer that opened onto the central courtyard. After setting her on her soggy tennis shoes, he grabbed her fists so she couldn't put them to use. "Settle down," he ordered, his hands clutching hers an effective deterrent.

For now.

He had a suspicion that when he finally let her go, she'd grab the wood ax and split his skull. "Listen, Wendy," he began as gently as his exasperation would allow. "You have to change out of those wet clothes. You're shivering. Then you need to get warm and you need to eat." He kept his expression, his tone, calm, as he worked to inject reason into this bizarre honeymoon. "We both need to keep our heads. We're alone here. You might as well face *that* fact and deal with it."

Her eyes blazed when he threw her own admonition back at her, but her expression exhibited more hopelessness than anger. She knew he was right. Like him, her days and nights alone in the woods, had taken their toll on her bravado. He could tell she was heartsick about having to make compromises with someone she considered lower than a worm's belly, but she wasn't stupid.

Expelling a ragged sigh, she nodded. Her arms relaxed within his grasp, and he sensed that if he let her go, she wouldn't fight. "Go upstairs and soak in a warm bath. I'll fix breakfast." He released her and her arms fell loosely to her sides.

Her jaw worked, but she made no move to strike out. He searched her eyes for some hint of softening, some rudimentary sign of tolerance. After a tension-filled minute, she spun away, dashing through the living room, toward the front stairs.

Dark irony curled his lips. "Congratulations, Raven.

You found out what you wanted to know,'' he muttered. ''Those eyes could cut diamonds.''

By the time she came downstairs, dressed in a sweatshirt, jeans and a pair of bulky socks, Josh had bathed and changed in a downstairs bathroom. Coincidentally, he, too, wore a sweatshirt, jeans and bulky socks. Odd how their choice of rainy-day attire was so simpatico, but as a couple they were as far apart as the North and South poles.

She'd pulled her damp hair back into a ponytail, and she wore no makeup. He wondered what he'd expected—that she'd doll herself up for him? Was the sack of guilt he'd been lugging around making him delusional? ''Hi.'' He smiled, hoping their cease-fire might be extended to civility. ''How's pancakes for breakfast? I have a batch ready, if you're hungry.''

She padded to the table and began to stroke Al on the head. The bird perched on the back of the chair nearest the window. ''How are you, my little traitor?'' Wendy murmured.

Thunder rumbled and Al *caw-cawed,* fidgeting sideways in a little hop-slide dance. ''I love *Josh!*'' the crow shrieked. ''I *love* Josh!''

Josh didn't turn, but continued to tend the pancakes. He'd already heard the newest addition to Alberta's repertoire. The first time the bird screeched the declaration, Wendy had been bathing after her aborted attempt to escape in the canoe. Alberta's timing had been as superbly faulty then as it was now.

With a melancholy hitch of his breath, he pictured Wendy, eyes alight, singing out that proclamation over and over during their two month engagement. Sadly, Al had picked it up with every melodious nuance of Wendy's speech patterns. By the time the crow displayed her newest mimic, Josh could take no pleasure in it. His emotions were too steeped in guilt, and hearing those words only worsened his burden.

He couldn't imagine what the sound of Al's fervent pronouncement must be doing to Wendy. He had a feeling her emotions ran heavily toward humiliation and homicide.

He cleared his throat. "Coffee's ready."

She didn't respond, so he glanced over his shoulder.

She stood at the window, shoulders stiff, staring out at the driving rain.

"Would you like a cup?"

She shook her head.

He experienced a twinge of aggravation. "Look, Wendy, you have to—"

"I want a divorce," she cut in quietly.

He heard it, and couldn't say he was surprised. Even so, it slugged him hard in the gut. Shifting to face the stovetop he shut his eyes and rubbed at his lids.

"Did you hear me?" she asked.

Reluctant to answer, he grimaced.

"Josh?"

"I heard you," he muttered.

Silence stretched into a slim, frayed thread. After a time, Josh pulled himself together, flipping the pancakes he no longer had any appetite for. A lot of things were going down the tubes with those four, blandly spoken words.

I want a divorce.

"I love *Josh!*" Alberta screeched in bird-brained disregard of the tension choking the room. "I *love* Josh! Roll me over in the clover, pretty boy."

"I'm going to roll you in breadcrumbs, bird, if you

don't button your beak,'' Josh mumbled under his breath.

He heard the flutter of wings, felt talons grip his shoulder. ''I love *Josh!* I *love* Josh!'' the bird repeated in what sounded disturbingly like Wendy's voice. ''*Kiss me,* pretty boy!''

Scowling at the bird, he removed her from his shoulder and set her on top of the refrigerator. ''Do you understand the phrase 'barbecued bird'?'' he ground out.

Flapping and cawing, Al hop-hopped around the surface, plainly unconcerned by the threat.

When Josh turned around, he was startled to see Wendy pouring herself a cup of coffee. She looked composed. When their eyes met, he saw nothing in the purple depths. No emotion at all. Not sadness, not anger, nothing. It was as though she'd stuffed everything in some deep, dark mental closet—anesthetizing her heart for the duration.

He stared, shaken. This dearth, this void of feeling, from such a vital woman, was utterly incompatible with the Wendy he knew. He swallowed the bile that had risen in his throat. ''Wendy?''

She walked casually to the table and took a seat before glancing his way. ''Yes?''

He shrugged to hide growing apprehension. ''I just...'' He moved to take the chair next to hers. ''Are you feeling okay?''

Her big eyes remained on him, but they didn't draw him in the way they used to. Where there had been loving invitation, he saw only blankness—an emotional wall—blocking access to her heart and mind. He was an outsider, now, a non-being in her world. It was simply her bad luck to be trapped with him in his isolated home in the woods.

He had a ferocious urge to pound his fists against that wall. He wanted back in, dammit! In there, with her, the world was decent and giving and loving. He didn't want to be shut out. He didn't want to be alone.

Bitter despair swept over him as his future without her loomed before his mind's eye—meaningless, cold and full of shadows. Wincing, he forced back the vision he didn't want to see, didn't want to believe.

In the flash of an instant came Joshua Raven's moment of truth. It struck him like the flat of a hand, hard, vicious, slapping him to wake to a new reality—one that completed him and made him whole.

All at once he understood why he'd allowed himself to go through with this crazy marriage conspiracy. He'd known it from the first moment he'd looked into those damn beautiful purple eyes, but he hadn't wanted to believe anything so sappy about himself. He'd always been Mr. Hardnose. Mr. Rational. Mr. There's-No-Such-Thing. Nothing so illusory as love could ever wield power over him.

Good Lord! What a fool he'd been! What a superficial, lost fool!

Instinctively he took her hand in both of his. ''Don't shut me out, Wendy,'' he implored, a throb in his voice. ''I love you.''

Joshua Raven had to be the cruelest man on earth. Those three words fell like burning coals on Wendy's heart, searing painful gashes she was hard-pressed to conceal. How dare he resort to such brutal tactics. She gulped down a sob and willed her eyes not to overflow with her misery. She would not listen to his lies, not be affected by him in any way—not the feel of his big, warm hands tenderly holding hers, and certainly not the stricken look in those lush, dark eyes. He was not only a dangerous corporate shark, he was a consummate actor. He actually looked distressed!

Her breath became a solid mass in her throat, and she couldn't breathe. Unable to bear the sweet torment of his touch an instant longer, she dragged her hand from his. "So you love me, now." Her voice was remarkably steady. Pushing herself to stand, she gripped the chair back to support wobbly legs.

With effort, she controlled the spasmodic shiver of loss and longing rushing through her. She knew if she didn't get out of his sight immediately she would explode into a wailing, shattered mess. Summoning a bland expression, she lifted a courageous chin. "It's fascinating how your love can be turned on and off like a faucet."

"Wendy." He reached again for her hand, but she side-stepped, moving out of range.

"Turn off the faucet, Josh." Incapable of meeting his gaze any longer, she whispered the bitterest lie of her life. "I—I don't love you anymore." Managing a stately grace only royalty or those determined not to collapse in anguish can achieve, she swept from the kitchen.

At the pantry entrance, Alberta lit on Wendy's shoulder. The bubble of gratitude that billowed inside her short-circuited her ability to remain composed, and tears flooded down her face. Hating the thought that Josh might discover how much she suffered, she fled to the master bedroom, locking herself and her pet inside.

Rain continued to fall long after the gloomy day died. Josh sat in darkness on the rough-hewn sofa in the living room. The rustic piece of furniture wasn't long enough for him to lie on, so he simply sat, listening to the rain, the thunder, and the creak of wood as Wendy paced the floor above his head.

She wasn't getting any sleep, either. Lolling his head back on the knotty-pine support, he willed her to come downstairs. He closed his eyes and concentrated. *Come to me. Look me in the eyes and tell me you don't love me.* He'd be damned if he'd let her out of his life now.

Wendy had become more than a minor obstacle in reaching his professional goal. Over the past two months she'd wangled her way into his heart to become a richly rewarding part of his life. A clean, pure presence, taming the gluttonous fire-breathing dragon of his soul. She'd given him so much—openly, honestly, trusting him with her gentle heart. And how had he repaid her? By stomping all over those delicate gifts with the hobnailed boots of his greed. He'd betrayed her trust, destroyed her faith.

How was he going to convince her he loved her, after all the harm he'd done?

He heard a click, and tensed. She was coming. She'd opened her door and was actually coming downstairs. Immobilized with surprise, he listened, tense and alert, following her progress in the darkness by sound alone. He sank back and drew in his feet, making him harder to detect in the blackness of the unlit house.

She reached the bottom of the stairs and turned toward the living room. He held his breath, barely able to make her out as she took the two steps down into the room. Without hesitation, without a glance in his direction, she turned toward the back of the house.

The kitchen. That's where she was going. She hadn't eaten all day. He knew she had no idea he was sitting there. No doubt she believed he was asleep in one of the three downstairs bedrooms. Evidently she had never peeked into any of them, or she would know they were completely unfurnished. The only bed in the place was in the master bedroom.

Once she disappeared through the back foyer, he stood and followed. When he reached the dining room, he detected light filtering through the pantry. He padded into the storeroom and moved soundlessly to the kitchen door, which stood ajar. Movement caught his eye and he located her as she opened the refrigerator. She wore the same sweatshirt and jeans she'd put on that morning. In the shaft of light, he checked his watch. Two o'clock. It seemed neither of them was getting much sleep. If the truth be told, he'd gotten more rest in the tree.

She took out the plate of sandwiches he'd made and set it on the countertop. After pouring a glass of milk, she padded to the table and sat down with her back to him. He experienced a tug of disappointment. He wanted to watch her face.

Stepping back, he leaned against the pantry counter, waiting as impatience gnawed at him. She needed to eat as much as he needed to find a way to convince her of his love. It was hard to stand there doing nothing after all the hours of waiting and listening, waiting and wanting. He burned to take her in his arms, beg her forgiveness, to show her the depth of his love in the world's most ancient and intimate form of communication.

What seemed like a year dragged by before Josh allowed himself to check on Wendy. She sat motionless, her hand clutching the glass of milk. He frowned at her lack of progress. *Please eat, darling.* He threw the thought at her, hoping the force of his will would prod her into action.

She lifted the glass to her mouth and his lips twitched with melancholy humor. If it were only that easy, his telepathic commands for her to believe him, to forgive him and love him, would have had her leaping into his arms hours ago, crying out, "I love *Josh!*" with the same fervor as Alberta's spirited rendition.

He heard the glass clank to the table. It was empty. Good. Usually, Wendy emptied her glass after finishing her food. Deciding it was as good a time as any, he pushed open the door and went into the kitchen.

Wendy was rising from her chair when she seemed to sense him and turned. She stilled, holding her plate and glass. Her expression registered surprise for a heartbeat, before that damnable mask of indifference settled over her features.

Without a word, she spun away, hurrying to the sink. She turned on the water and rinsed her plate, making it grimly obvious she intended to ignore him. When she lifted the dinner plate to transfer it into the dishwasher, he was beside her, taking hold of it. "Did I ever tell you about the man I bought this place from?"

He plucked the wet dish from her grip. Instead of answering his question, she went about rinsing the glass.

"He was a Texas oil millionaire. Actually I bought it from his estate lawyer," Josh went on, refusing to allow her snub to discourage him. "As the story goes, the Texan built this place as a retirement home for himself and his wife. They'd moved in and were still decorating the place when she suddenly died." Josh took the glass from her hands, though she was still diligently scrubbing it beneath the spray of water. "He left the place exactly the way it was when his wife died. Never did another thing. Never built a boathouse, never bought a boat. I understand he stayed here, all alone, nursing his broken heart until the day he died." Josh stuck the glass in the dishwasher and closed it. "This place hasn't known much happiness, Wendy. I hope—"

"What sort of provision did Daddy put in your contract about divorce?" Wendy interrupted, her voice cool.

Her dogged single-mindedness on the subject of divorce irked him. He gritted his teeth and counted to ten. "There was no provision made in our deal about a divorce."

She met his gaze, her big eyes displaying disbelief. "Come now. In this day and age? You don't expect me to swallow that. What do you have to give up if I leave you?"

He inhaled a quick breath, then let it out with a slow shake of his head. "Nothing," he said, truthfully.

She frowned, scoffing, "I wouldn't believe that in a million years!"

"Your mother didn't divorce your father, and I had no reason to believe you would divorce me."

Her expression grew incredulous. "You had no reason—*how vain can you be?* Did you really assume you were so perfect no woman could ever want to leave you?"

Her taunt stung. Over the years, he'd had quite a bit of experience with women, and never once had anyone dumped him. Perhaps there had been a touch of conceit in the oversight. Clearly Gower's raging ego, and his history with his own wife, had blinded him to how different his daughter was from her mother. At the time the bargain was made, Joshua hadn't even met the lady.

In truth, when Gower made no mention of a divorce clause, Josh had been surprised, but elected not to mention it. After all, as the contract stood, divorce or no, the company was his. So why make problems for himself? Besides, his intentions had been honorable even if their deal hadn't been. Josh's plans were to make a home with

Wendy, start his overdue family, and get on with his greatly enhanced corporate life.

"It seems I was wrong to think you wouldn't want to leave me," he murmured, deciding to keep explanations to a minimum.

"It *seems* you were wrong? *Ha!*" Her facade of indifference cracked as anguish edged her voice. "You should have that carved on your tombstone!"

"Perhaps," he said. "But I'm being honest with you, Wendy."

"Honest!" Her eyes glistened, and he felt a rush of exhilaration. She was giving him back her emotions, at least. Lord, he wished he could get her trust and her sweet kisses back as readily. But he was no fool. He knew it would take time to prove himself. Honesty was the path back.

"A divorce won't do me any harm," he admitted. "Besides, you don't want to leave." He couldn't stop himself from taking her hand. "You love me and we both know it."

She yanked free and shoved at his chest. "I don't believe you about the business. You're saying that to trick me, make me think you have nothing to lose."

A hot current of blood swept up his neck and burned his face. His gaze locked with hers. *I have a lot to lose, darling,* he vowed with his eyes. *I'll lose you.* He knew it would do no good to repeat his pledge of love. Not now. She couldn't believe anything he said at present. Only time and patience would disclose if he could ever win back her confidence. And though he knew, deep in his soul, that she loved him, he also knew she would never again give herself to him, freely and openly—not without complete, uncompromising trust.

"I'm going to bed." She headed for the pantry exit.

"Good idea." He fell in step behind her.

She cocked her head to peer around. "Don't follow me."

He shrugged his hands into his jeans pockets. "Do you expect me to sleep in the kitchen?"

She scowled and spun away. "I don't care where you sleep!"

With a surge of wry amusement, he murmured, "I have a feeling you will."

"Ha!" She marched through the dining room, the back foyer and living room. When she reached the foot of the stairs, she wheeled on him. "I told you not to follow me! Where are you going?"

"To bed." He put a hand on the pine rail and smiled. "Ignore me."

"No problem!" With a haughty toss of her head, she stomped up the steps.

She reached the master bedroom, storming inside, but his hand on the door kept her from slamming it. "What do you think you're doing?"

He slipped inside and closed the door at his back. "Are you having trouble with your memory, darling?" He indicated the bed with a nod. "I told you twice."

Apparently it didn't take a brick to fall on her to figure out what he meant, because her lips sagged open. "Not in *my* bed, you're not!"

He lounged against the door. "*Your* bed?"

Even in the darkness, he could see her throat go into a spasm of swallows. "Okay—you're too big for me to stop you. I'll take one of the others."

"Others?" Speculating on how long it would take her to grasp the significance of the word, he let it linger in the stillness. While he waited, he crossed his arms before him.

"What do you mean?" She looked unsure.

"Remember, I told you about the Texas oil millionaire? How his wife died and how he stopped decorating the house?"

There was another taut pause. "He never furnished the other bedrooms," she mumbled as though stating a very unpalatable fact.

"Right."

"But—but you could sleep on the couch."

"Nope. I tried."

"Then, I will."

He didn't enjoy the resolve in her voice. "Of course, you may," he stated, his manner deliberately arrogant.

She had cast her gaze away, but at his supercilious tone, her head jerked up. "I—what?"

He lifted a brow, projecting a thoroughly overbearing attitude. He knew he was manipulating her as completely now as at any time in their past, but he prayed his motives would excuse him. How could he show her his love if they were never in the same room? He wanted her within arm's length, touching distance, so that deep in the night he could take her into his arms.

He wanted her to remember what they'd so briefly shared, to see that she didn't want a divorce. No matter how underhandedly she'd become Mrs. Joshua Raven, their marriage was right. She had to see that. He had to make her see. "You have my permission to sleep on the couch," he told her with as much masterful impertinence as he could stomach.

"I have your *permission,* huh?" She glared at him for a split second before she whirled away. Yanking her sweatshirt off over her head, she hurled it to the floor. She wore nothing underneath and even though her back was to him, Josh felt an immediate physical effect.

Yanking open the snap at her waist, she unzipped her jeans and shimmied out of them. Though she wore panties, the sight, even in darkness, was disturbing.

She reached for something draped over the log footboard and dragged it on. "Thank you very much, Mr. Raven!" she jeered. "But as far as I'm concerned you can march your egotistical patoot downstairs and sleep on the couch, even if you have to bend yourself into a pretzel. You don't have any right to give me orders! As long as I'm Mrs. Raven, I can sleep anyplace in this back-country mausoleum I want!"

He was glad he was resting against the door, because the sight of her slim, pale body made him light-headed. He hadn't expected nudity. Even that brief flash in the darkness had done him damage. *Hell,* the woman knew how to punch a guy right where it hurt.

Suffering behind his carefree pose, he sucked in a restorative breath. As he gradually released it, Wendy scrambled under the covers and flipped to face away from him.

For a long moment, his gaze lingered on the mound of covers that outlined his bride. With a certain amount of melancholy, he considered his latest handiwork, far from proud of himself. But he hadn't gotten where he was in life without being able to read people, to correctly judge how they would react when steered into certain positions. If there was one thing he'd learned about Wendy, it was the fact that she couldn't abide being told what she could and couldn't do. By giving her his lordly permission to sleep on the couch, he'd pushed a hot button that wouldn't allow her to do it—even if it meant she would be sleeping with him.

He knew his superior attitude would so enrage her that

she wouldn't be able think the thing through. He knew she expected him to go downstairs and sleep on the couch.

"Not likely, sweetheart," he whispered.

CHAPTER TEN

OSH knew Wendy wasn't asleep. She lay there, motion-
ess, waiting for him to leave. *Well, sweetheart, you're
oing to have a long wait.* Pushing away from the door,
e walked to the side of the bed and sat down. He had
hrugged out of his sweatshirt before he felt movement.

"What are you doing?" Wendy's voice was high-
itched and worried.

He undid the button fastener at his waistband before
hifting to look at her. She had drawn up on one elbow
nd was clutching the covers to her breast like a shield.
urning away, he continued to unfasten his jeans, slip-
ing one brass button at a time. *Don't get up! He com-
nanded mentally. Don't leave me! Please!*

"I'm going to bed," he said at last, then cleared his
hroat. His voice sounded a little husky to be convinc-
ngly offhand. Deciding he'd better tack on something
o appease her, he added, "It's a big bed, Wendy. I just
vant to get some sleep, okay?"

She made no move, said nothing, so he decided the
ituation was as tolerable as it was likely to get.
tanding, he slipped out of his jeans then slid under the
overs, careful to make no abrupt or aggressive moves.
Ie wanted her there, beside him. He needed her there.

Facing away from her, he settled in, listening. She
adn't moved, but that didn't necessarily mean things
vere going well. She must still be poised on one elbow.
robably trying to decide what to do.

"I can use the bedroll." She didn't sound as resolve as she had before.

He closed his eyes and petitioned the heavens to giv him a break he didn't deserve. "The bedroll's outsid Wendy." He opened his eyes. "Don't be afraid of m I would never hurt you."

Thunder burst around them like raucous applaus Josh frowned, positive she'd begun to speak before h words were obscured by the noise. "What?"

He felt movement, and his breathing seized up in h chest.

"I said, you've already hurt me."

The movement stopped, but she was still in bed. W it possible she'd merely lay back down? Did he deser his luck?

"You've done a lot of nasty things, Josh, but I don believe you would take a woman against her will." H despondent sigh filled the room. "I'm not happy abo this, but I'm too exhausted to fight."

Powerful relief filled him and he could breathe agai "Thank you."

"Just stay where you are!"

The beginnings of a smile twitched at the corners his mouth.

Wendy knew she was a sick puppy. At least when came to Joshua Raven, she was anything but sensib She'd lain there as still as a stump for hours, unable sleep. His scent filled her head; his radiant heat reach out, warming, beckoning.

At least she'd been wise enough to turn her back him. She didn't know what the added onslaught of se ing him in repose might do to her—forced to stare those wide, tanned shoulders, to witness the sinful thic ness of his lashes fanned out across high, handsome cheekbones. And a mere glimpse at those big, gentle hands made her melt. Memories flooded back of those hands, so skilled in pleasure-giving. She squeezed her eyes shut, attempting to block out visions, sensations she feared would not fade, even with the largess of time.

Somewhere in the night, he reached for her. Whether waking or sleeping, she didn't know. He had drawn her against him, taking her into his embrace—but nothing more. If he had begun to fondle her or make undue advances, she might have gathered enough outrage to resist, to push him away. But he did nothing but hold her, enfolding her within the hollow of his body.

The night was cold, the fire long dead. His touch was bracing, ironic succor to her battered soul. She knew she should pull free, dash away to safety, but her heart would have none of it. To her foolish heart, this man represented a safe haven, all the shelter she needed from life's storms.

Oh, why was her heart so fallible, so easily taken in? Why had her naive, silly heart given her over to him, body and soul, leaving her no escape? Why did she lie in his arms, delighting in the feel of his hard, male body pressed against her back? And why did her fingers seek out the wedding ring he wore, her spirit soaring in gladness at the feel of that flesh-warmed band of gold.

How was she going to convince her heart that everything she'd thought was real between them had been a lie? The ring he wore had nothing to do with loving her. The reasons he'd asked her to marry him had nothing to do with who Wendy Isaac was—as a person. Only as a bloodless stepping stone to his goal.

Held in his arms this way, Wendy could conjure up no anger, just wave after wave of sadness. As crazy as it seemed, she kissed the ring, snuggling her cheek against his hand. How long she dared stay in his arms, she didn't know. She only knew she didn't have the courage or will to break free—yet.

His breath feathered her hair in slow, regular intervals; his heartbeat resounded through her, its tempo solid and unchanging. Cuddling her in his embrace, Josh slept like an innocent, as though he didn't have a care in the world.

She wished desperately sleep would come to her, too—untainted, immaculate, sleep—without disturbing thoughts and haunting memories. She wished she could loathe Josh. And she wished she could drive him out of her heart and her mind. Yet here she was, a stupid, lovesick ninny, snuggled within the harbor of his body, reluctant even to drive him from her bed.

Josh woke slowly, his first groggy observation was that it was daylight. The second—he was alone. That realization brought him fully awake. His last conscious thought before falling into the first restful sleep he'd had in days was that Wendy was in his arms.

He stared at the side of the bed where she had been, experiencing a sharp snap-kick to the gut. Pushing up, he was about to throw off the covers when he saw her. She was curled in the rocking chair, wearing his robe and staring into the flames of a revived fire.

"Good morning." He shifted to lounge on one elbow, his mood lifting measurably. She was still there. "Nice fire."

She cast him a narrowed glance. "I was cold."

He watched her with a masculine hunger that astonished him. She sat there, made rosy by the firelight, looking cuddly and exciting all at once. She was so beautiful he was shocked that he hadn't seen it right away. He'd been a fool in a lot of ways until his Odd-Miss-Isaac slipped unnoticed into his heart. Unable to help himself, he smiled. "I'm sorry you're cold. You felt warm to me."

She jerked around to stare at him. Correction, it was more of a glare—if a frightened doe could glare. "What do you mean, I felt warm to you?"

He watched the sparks of indignation brighten her gaze, and struggled to master the impulse to make love to her right there on the rug. "Are you sure you want to go there, darling?" he murmured. "You're not the best liar in the world."

She stiffened and one slender leg shot from the bundle of white terry. Only her toes touched the floor, but he could tell she was poised for flight. "Lying is something you know plenty about, isn't it!"

Her accusation sliced deep, but he knew he deserved it. The impulse to reach out and touch her face, smooth away the sadness, was almost palpable. Knowing she wouldn't stand for physical contact, he crushed the bed-covers in his fist.

"Anyway, I—I wasn't awake!" she insisted haltingly. "I mean, I don't know what you're talking about."

He pushed up to sit, trying to keep his expression composed. But he was sure the look in his eyes told a different story. All she need do was meet his gaze to see how much her nearness staggered him. Something sub-tle, yet wonderful, had happened to her in the past few days. The dormant sexuality of her body had been aroused, and now she fairly radiated a sensuous aura.

If he hadn't known her as well as he did, he would surely believe she was playing the hard-to-get game with purpose—to turn him into a blubbering, broken fool. He wondered if she had any idea what degree of power a woman had over the man who loved her.

Slipping his legs from beneath the covers he reached for his jeans and pulled them on. Fastening all the buttons except the waistband, he glanced her way again. She was eyeing him with uncertainty. He experienced absurd humor at that. She was uncertain. He was downright whipped.

Cautiously he entered her personal space, kneeling beside the rocker and placing a hand near hers on the arm of the chair. ''Thank you for last night,'' he whispered. ''For whatever reason—awake or asleep, fluke or fate—thank you.'' He grazed her hand with his thumb, but she jerked away.

She pulled her leg back up into the cocoon of terry and pointedly faced the fire. Her body language told him one thing, but the fact that she was still there, still curled like a kitten so close, told him something else. She was fighting her attraction. He prayed she was losing. She loved him, dammit! And he loved her. They could make this marriage work. If she would only let herself see that.

''Wendy, what can I do?'' he asked, his body throbbing with male hunger. He wanted her and he wanted her to want him.

''Get me out of here.''

Her request was like the flick of a whip, splitting flesh. In the electric silence that followed he cast his gaze toward the fire, powerless. ''I can't,'' he whispered.

She jumped up. ''I can *not* believe all the stupid things I did for you!'' His gaze shot to hers. Puzzled at her meaning, he stared as she glowered at him. ''I wore that stupid black dress. I went to all those insufferable parties! I turned myself into a vapid little twit for you. I neglected my literacy students, my duties at the animal shelter gift shop. And the library! I—I even held you close when I *thought* you had your—your problem! And all the time you just didn't want—*couldn't stand the idea of making love to me!*'' Her vehemence, and the deep wound he could see in her eyes, chilled his blood.

''Lord, Wendy, it wasn't like that. I hated those parties, too, and I never asked you to change for me. As for not sleeping with you, I thought it would be more honorable to wait.''

''But you were fine with it, weren't you!''

He shook his head. Hating this. ''I didn't think—''

''Don't give me that!'' she spat. ''You were thinking all the time! You were manipulating and plotting and fast-talking! I was happy as a lark being a blind, stupid idiot. I'm ashamed to say I let my heart do all my thinking.'' Her voice broke and Josh looked on helplessly as she pulled herself together. ''Knowing you has taught me an important lesson, Mr. Raven,'' she charged. ''I won't make the mistake of falling for a handsome face, *ever again.* I won't be so quick to believe any old line just because it's honey-coated and pleasant to swallow.''

She plunked her hands on her hips. ''See? Our little association hasn't been a total waste.'' Her voice wavered, but her eyes remained locked with his in open warfare. ''I'd be curious to know what you've learned, if anything?'' She cocked her head and smiled at him, but murder lurked beneath that show of teeth.

He slowly stood, holding her gaze. ''I learned about love.''

''Ha!'' she shrieked.

Shoving both hands through her hair she mussed it further. In the fire's brilliance, Wendy became the image of a siren gone mad, a sexy nymph bent on man's destruction—not with the mythical lure of love, but with the total eradication of it. She had the power. All she need do to turn him into pulp was open that robe. Display for him all the beauty and sweetness he couldn't have.

"I know I don't deserve it, Wendy, but please believe me."

She laughed, an unsettling hysterical note dancing around the edges. "Sure, why not?" she scoffed. "I believe you love me, Josh. Just like I believe my father will win the Miss America pageant." She flounced around to face away from him, throwing up her hands theatrically. "I believe Sylvester Stallone is really an eighty-five-year-old grandmother with a good makeup man. And I believe every time a husband says *'Sure I'm listening, honey,'* to his wife, he really is!" She laughed again. "Unfortunately for you, I'm a naive lunatic!"

"Wendy, don't—"

"Don't what?" she cut in, wheeling on him. "Don't rain on your parade? Don't do this to you? Don't screw up the best deal you ever made in your life?" she charged, tightly. "Don't *what?*"

"Don't put yourself down," he said quietly. "You're a beautiful woman. Any man would be lucky to have you."

She stared, eyes narrowing. Her anger fairly sizzled in the air, singeing him. "*Don't...*" she began, but her sentence died, and she spun away. "You're not being fair," she cried weakly, as though trying to catch her breath. "Take your medicine like a man. Your trick didn't work and you've lost. Now just leave me alone."

Her plea came out barely above a whisper. Josh sensed she was on the verge of breaking down, and he wanted to hold her. But he'd already told her he wasn't losing anything if she left him. She was deep into denial.

;he wouldn't let herself see that she loved him and she vouldn't believe he loved her, even if he burned the vords into his chest with a fireplace poker.

He swallowed to ease the ache in his throat. "Okay." 'urning away, he grabbed his sweatshirt. "Have it your vay. I'm a pig and a liar." He headed toward the door. Vhen he got there he turned back. "So what do you vant for breakfast?"

She flicked him a glance and he could see tears shimnering on her lower lashes. "Is that all you have to say? 'ou're a pig, and what do I want for breakfast?"

His options exhausted, at least for now, he lounged gainst the door and shrugged. "You heard me."

"I see." A tear escaped down her cheek, yet she manged to lift her chin in defiance. "In that case, I want *ork* for breakfast."

osh separated the bacon slices in the skillet, concenating on the delicious smell and the sizzle. He'd done verything he could think of to convince Wendy of his eelings. He exhaled, startled by how much like a groan sounded. All he had on his side was time. This was 'riday. He had just over a week left alone with her to et her to change her mind about a divorce.

A sound that had nothing to do with cooking bacon rew his attention. A fluttering. The noise was followed wiftly by the bite of talons in his left shoulder. He cast is feathered companion a sidelong smirk. "And a painıl good morning to you, Alberta." He stabbed a limp iece of bacon with his cooking fork and lifted it. 'Would you care for pork for breakfast, too?"

The crow nipped at his ear.

"Hey, bird!" he groused. "I meant the pork in the *an.*"

"I love *Josh!*" Al crooned. "I *love* Josh!"

"Yeah? Well, you're the only one," he muttered. A sudden thought hit, and he squinted at the bird. "Al, ol girl, could you do something for me?"

"*Kiss me,* pretty boy!"

"Not in this life, sweetcakes." He angled his hea around to better see the bird. "Repeat after me—Jos loves Wendy," he whispered softly. "Josh love Wendy."

Al whispered back, "Kiss me, pretty boy."

Eyeing the ceiling with a mixture of frustration an wry humor, Josh repeated, "Josh loves Wendy."

"I love *Josh!*"

"No. Josh loves Wendy."

"Let's scram!" Al said in a hushed mimic of Josh' whisper. "It's the cops."

He couldn't help himself, and laughed. "You bir brain."

"You birdbrain—*caw-caw!*"

Josh shook his head. "I give up."

"You birdbrain!" Al screeched. "Roll me over in th clover you birdbrain!"

"Now I'm a pig and a birdbrain. That's just great. Josh grumbled, absently tending the bacon. "They' both suitable, but would you mind shutting up about it?

"Josh loves Wendy," Al whispered.

Josh stilled. "You did it!" Laying aside his fork, h dislodged the bird from his shoulder and brought h around to look squarely into her little pink eyes. "S it again. Say, 'Josh loves Wendy.' But louder."

"Louder, you birdbrain!"

He grimaced, eyeing the obstinate fowl with disa proval. "You're hopeless." Setting Al on top of the r frigerator, he muttered, "You belong in a pie with twenty-three other crows."

"*Louder,* you birdbrain!"

Josh turned back to the stove, contrary laughter rumbling in his chest. He was about the least happy man in the universe, but that blasted bird brought such an absurd twist to his world, he couldn't help being distracted by it.

His smile died when he realized Wendy did much the same thing. She brought a uniqueness into his existence—a warmth, an off-beat humor. Traits he'd discovered he needed. He'd lived in a bloodless, grasping world much too long. Almost too long to be saved. If Wendy left him, he feared his last hope of salvation might disappear with her.

"Let's scram. It's the cops," Al whispered. The warning drew Josh's attention because it sounded awkwardly like a seduction—in his own voice.

"Birdbrain," he said. "If you can't get it right, just shut up."

"If she can't get what right?"

Josh hadn't heard Wendy come in. She must be wearing those blasted, quiet socks again. He removed the last strip of bacon to a plate covered with a paper towel for draining off the grease. "Nothing," he gritted. "How would you like your eggs?"

"I can cook my own eggs."

"That's not what I asked," he said, growing annoyed. Why couldn't the woman slack off for a single minute?

He knew she had walked up beside him before he saw her; her fresh-from-the-tub scent filled his nostrils, a tastier aroma, by far, than the bacon. He turned, taking her in, but she refused to look in his direction. Instead, she plucked the fork from his hands. "Or would you rather cook yours first?"

Irritated by her bull-headedness, he ran a hand over his mouth to keep from saying something that would make him more *persona non grata* than he already was. "I'll make coffee."

Once he got the percolator perking, he walked back to where she stood before the stove. His glance at the skillet gave him pause. It was full to overflowing with frying eggs. He counted. "Eight? That should clog an artery or two."

She blinked, seeming to come out of a trance. "What?"

He indicated the pan. "Your breakfast. You must have a thing for cholesterol."

Frowning in what appeared to be confusion, she looked at the pan. Josh watched as her cheeks grew peachy. He felt a tug of desire at the sight. "Oh..." She flicked him a brief, almost guilty look. "I guess I lost track."

"I guess." He suppressed a wry grin. "I'd better get these out before they turn into roofing tiles. Move, sweetheart." He gently nudged her with his hip. "If you don't mind I'll have some of yours."

She cast him a quick glance. "I suppose we shouldn't waste food." She took a couple of plates down from a shelf.

"No, we've got another week here." Taking up a spatula he scooped the eggs onto a platter. "Too many roofing tiles and we might start to get hungry."

"I suppose you're blaming me for all this." Petulance wrinkled her brow. "I broke the phone, so we're stuck! Is that what you're saying?"

"No, Wendy." He took the plates from her, laying them aside. "I don't blame you for anything."

She glowered at him for a few seconds, opening her mouth and closing it. Finally, in a drawn-out groan, she cried, "Why won't you fight with me?" She lifted her fists, shaking them under his nose. "Fight with me, Josh. Say hurtful, nasty things to me. I want to leave here hating you with all my heart!"

"Are you saying you don't hate me that way, now?"

With a wail of frustration, she pounded his chest. "I do! I do hate you!" Her voice became a faulty whimper. "I hate you—oh, I *want* to..." Suddenly her hands were no longer fisted. Her arms slid about his neck. She pressed against him, her trembling lips brushing his throat as she pleaded, "Make me hate you! I've tried—I've tried so hard!"

Icy self-loathing twisted around his heart, and he gathered her in his arms. "I'm sorry, darling."

"No—*no!*" She lifted her face to snag his gaze. "No—say something cruel. Tell me you don't love me. Tell me all the reasons why! Tell me you think I'm silly and strange and you'll be glad to get rid of me." She buried her face in his chest as a sob burst from her throat. Her body trembled with anguish.

He locked her within his embrace. "I love you, Wendy," he whispered, ruffling her sweet-smelling hair. "I can't do what you ask. It would be a lie."

Laughter gurgled in her throat, sad and overwrought. "You're a fiend! Holding on to me this way!" She lifted her face again, looking so distraught a wave of nausea swept through him. "Be kind. For once in your selfish life, Joshua Raven," she begged brokenly, "be—be kind. *Please.*"

Her suffering was so intense, it did him physical harm.

His heart constricted, crushed in the vise of her tearful plea. But he couldn't say those things about her. They weren't true. It was wrong. Wrong for both of them.

She loosened her deathgrip, and he realized she was looking at him again. He sensed she could see in his eyes that he had no intention of helping her hate him. "No, sweetheart." His arms tightened about her and he wished he could pull her inside himself. Keep her safe, make her the most important part of him. "No." He gazed down at her, his resolve unshakable. "Never."

Refusing to consider the right or wrong of it, he claimed her lips with his, hungrily covering her mouth. He moved his lips across hers, devouring, exploring. The velvety soft, sweet coupling sang through his veins, warmed his insides, made him whole.

He groaned, wanting more, wanting all. Gently coaxing, he parted her lips, eager to deepen the physical expression of his love.

Victory seemed within his grasp when he heard a feral cry. Wendy wrenched her face from his, pressing impotently against his chest. "Let me go!" she implored feebly. "You—you have no heart!"

Disoriented by her sudden, violent invective, he released her, his body weak and on fire. Sagging against the counter, he stared at her. In bizarre slow motion he watched her fists batter impotently at his chest, felt the dull thud-thud-thud as she acted out her bitter frustration. It seemed unreal, far away. He was incapacitated, numb, an outsider witnessing as his world spun perilously out of orbit.

Like an automaton, he grasped her wrists, halting her ineffectual attack. She was saying something—probably shouting it by the look on her tear-stained face. He couldn't hear her. It seemed he'd gone deaf, too.

He frowned, trying to make out her words. But did it really matter? He knew what she was saying. Maybe, by some ironic quirk of fate, this last bit of lunacy—his kiss—had pushed her over the edge. Maybe now, she truly did hate him.

But hate between them wasn't for the best. Hate was all wrong. He knew it in his soul, yet there was nothing he could do to fix it. He'd screwed up his chance at happiness. All he had now was his work, which suddenly seemed like a barren, lonely destiny.

He hardly registered the fact when she wrenched her wrists from his grasp. An instant later something blinded him, snapping him out of his paralyzed stupor. By the smell and greasy feel, he realized he was covered with lukewarm eggs. Peeling one of the slimy disks away from his eyes, he could see that Wendy was gone.

"Josh loves Wendy," Al whispered.

Leaning heavily against the counter, Josh looked at the bird, murder and a little yolk in his eye.

On the one-week anniversary of his wedding day, Josh woke up alone in his big bed. He opened his eyes to an overcast, gray day, perfect for his mood. Last night Wendy had adamantly announced that she planned to sleep on the couch—*alone.* He'd made a fire for her in the living room hearth, then left her to her privacy.

Blast it! Without her beside him he'd slept badly when he'd slept at all. Why did he have to be holding Wendy in his arms to get any real rest? He knew exactly why. *He had it bad.* Lying on his back, he slipped his hands beneath his head and glared at the ceiling. He had it bad, all right. Love was an insidious condition. It crept up on a man and had him in a stranglehold before he knew what the hell was wrong with him.

Considering Wendy's attitude lately, he hoped there was a cure. But as far as his stubborn, purple-eyed little bride was concerned, he had serious doubts. Which was okay, too. Josh had never been a man to accept defeat. He had a week left on this honeymoon, and *by heaven,* he didn't plan to squander it.

He heard a scratching sound and eyed Al's covered cage. The darn bird had whispered "Josh loves Wendy" several times yesterday, but, naturally, *never* when Wendy was within earshot. "Darn bird," he muttered.

Another sound invaded the stillness, but it didn't register. He frowned. Al scratched again. "Okay, okay," Josh mumbled. "I'll let you out in a minute."

He concentrated on the sound. A low whirring—no a rumbling. Like a faraway engine.

His eyes went wide and he bolted up to sit. "A boat." But it sounded like it was leaving. Leaving? Vaulting from the bed, he grabbed his jeans and struggled into them, hopping and stumbling out of the room. *The mail boat, he'd bet anything on it.* It must have been delivering a letter from somebody.

When he reached the bottom of the stairs, the door stood ajar. Skidding to a halt, he glanced toward the living room. Wendy wasn't there. The bedcovers had been tossed on the floor, as though in haste.

Alarmed, the truth exploded in his brain. "Oh, my lord," he breathed, sprinting out the door. He saw it off in the distance. The motorboat employed by the U.S. mail—leaving the inlet.

He tore down the granite walkway, waving and shouting, but the vessel was too far away for him to be heard over its engine. When he reached the dock, he ran all the way to the end, knowing it was futile, but unable to stop.

A letter lay there. More out of reflex than interest, he picked it up. It looked like a greeting card. The envelope was blue and it was addressed to Mr. and Mrs. Joshua Raven. The return address held the faintly scrawled name "Judy Sawyer." She must have gotten that job. Hadn't Wendy insisted Judy let her know immediately? It was somehow fitting that Wendy's kindness and selfless interest in others had come to her aid in her escape from the husband she loathed.

Loathed! his mind jeered. *The woman you love beyond all else in the world loathes you! Congratulations!*

Despair welled up in his throat like a fist. His breathing shallow and labored, he lifted his gaze, staring as the motorboat disappeared around an outcropping of rock. *His Wendy, his love, his heart, was leaving on that boat.*

Misery slammed into his gut with the force of a combat boot. Unsteady, he sat down. Blankly, he looked out over the calm waters. Only the barest traces of the mail boat's wake were visible now.

Gone. Wendy was gone. Time was no longer on his side. She had run away from him, taking nothing with her but the clothes on her back. She hadn't even dared fetch her beloved Al. That's how desperately she'd wanted to get away.

He swallowed, his throat scratchy dry. He'd read somewhere that in times of extreme crisis, the body shuts down all unessential functions in its fight for survival. The throat going dry was one sign. He gritted his teeth at the insight. Evidently his entire body knew how fundamental Wendy was to his emotional survival. He'd shut himself down, investing all his energy, funneling his attention, into his mad, headlong race to stop her.

He looked at his hands. They trembled badly. He

coiled them into fists as memories surged back—of how her skin warmed in the throes of passion, of the simple, loving touch of her fingers entwined with his. How could he have known two months ago that he would fall so deeply in love with a young woman who wore a crow like an Easter bonnet and believed that a person who couldn't read was one of life's greatest tragedies?

How could he have guessed that losing her—just as he discovered the precious gift she was—would be *his* greatest tragedy?

CHAPTER ELEVEN

"THERE you are, girl!"

Wendy's heart dropped as her father loomed at the top of the staircase in her apartment building. His face was so red he looked in danger of blowing the top of his head into outer space. She faltered on the step. She'd spent the last two weeks avoiding him, hiding in the library basement compiling information on donated books into the computer. She knew she should have confronted her father right away, but she also knew it would only turn into a shouting match. She didn't have the energy yet. Her wounds were still too raw to charge into another battle.

"When Josh got back to town he phoned to tell me you'd run away!" Gower shouted, his tone heavy with accusation.

Gathering her courage, Wendy made quick work of the rest of the steps. "Let's go inside, Daddy. The whole world doesn't need to hear this."

"I don't care who hears, girl," he bellowed. "You just march yourself back to your husband, do you understand me?"

She kept her jaws clamped to keep from shouting at her father. How dare he suggest she go back to a man who'd bought her as part of a package deal! Digging around in her purse, she located her keys. Her fingers didn't seem to want to cooperate, and she dropped the key ring twice before successfully unlocking her door.

Tugging her father inside, she turned on him, her temper flaring. "I won't go back! You know how I feel about marriage for profit, Dad. But you tricked me, anyway—you and—and Joshua Raven! I won't be a piece of property like my mother!"

A vein pulsed in Gower's temple, and his jowls clumped as though he were gnashing his teeth. "Raven proposed to you in good faith."

"Good faith to you, not to me!" She spun away, tossing her purse on the couch, then turned back, hurt bubbling to the surface. "*Why* Daddy—why did you leave that note in his briefcase? Was it because you couldn't stand not being absolutely sure I understood I'd been manipulated? Did your ego require that I know? That I *suffer?* What shameful, Machiavellian reasoning made you write that down? Can't you stand to see anybody happy—even if it's nothing but a self-deluded happiness?"

"What are you talking about?" he growled. "How dare you make me out some kind of a sadistic creature."

"You are—you *and* Joshua Raven. You're greedy killer sharks, and I wish you both all the happiness and success you deserve." She pointed toward the door. "Now get out. I'm tired of trying to make a family out of the two of us. To be honest, Daddy, I don't care if I ever see you again!"

His florid face went purple and his eyes bulged. "I won't have you giving me orders. I can cut off your funds, like that." He snapped his squat fingers. "You may live like an urchin, giving all your money to those sentimental charities, but you still need to eat!"

"I'll eat." She stared him down. "I have a standing offer to run the Literacy Center. That's a paid position. I don't need mother's inheritance."

He harrumphed. "You're a stiff-backed headstrong

neophyte. You have no idea who you're dealing with. I'll crush you for your treachery. Don't think I won't!"

"*My* treachery?" She couldn't hold back a harsh, forlorn laugh. "How can you say that with a straight face? Get out of my home!" Stomping to the door, she threw it wide. "Now."

He stormed by her swathed in a cloud of pungent cologne. She made a face at the spicy-sweet stench, slamming the door after him. She felt ill and pressed her hand to her stomach. Woozy, she clung to the doorknob to keep from stumbling. After a minute, she staggered to the couch and sank down, wondering what had come over her. Fights with her father had never made her light-headed and sick, before. Hunching forward, she dropped her face in her hands, biting back a sob.

Why couldn't her father love her? Why did he idolize the gods of wealth and power over everything and everyone else? And why did she ache with longing for Josh—a man as flawed and superficial as her father?

The ringing of the phone made her jump. She lifted her face from her hands, sniffling. She didn't want to answer, but out of habit she leaned over to the end table and picked up the receiver. "Hello?" She was gratified she only sounded tired.

"Mrs. Raven?" came a businesslike, female voice.

Her heart lurched at the reminder that she was still Josh's wife—though in name only. "Y-yes."

"I'm Faith Hanfield, an attorney on Mr. Raven's legal staff. I called to see if you're free tonight. There are some papers he would like you to sign."

She closed her eyes and slumped back. She hadn't been able to bring herself to initiate divorce proceedings. Apparently Joshua felt no similar reluctance. "Of course—the divorce."

"Well—yes." The lawyer sounded both apologetic and businesslike. "Would eight o'clock be convenient?"

"Tonight?" Panic rushed through Wendy, and that surprised her. Divorce was what she wanted.

"If that's not convenient—"

"No—no, it's fine," she broke in, telling herself it was time to face reality. A one-sided love was worse than no love at all. "I'll expect you at eight. Do you need the address?"

"Mr. Raven gave it to me."

"I see." Wendy felt empty. Her head swam and she rubbed her eyes. "Fine—fine. I'll look forward to it." She grimaced. How lame! How absurdly untrue.

The phone went dead as the attractive-sounding attorney hung up. Listlessly, Wendy replaced the receiver in its cradle. "Goodbye, Miss—whatever," she mumbled.

Leave it to Josh to have a pretty lady lawyer serve her with divorce papers!

The knock at her door startled Wendy awake. She lay on her couch with an ice pack on her head. She didn't feel well. Lifting her arm, she checked her watch. Seven forty-five. The attorney, Faith Hanfield, was more than punctual. "Just a minute." She dropped the ice pack on the coffee table. When she sat up, it took her a few seconds to clear her head. Obviously she was coming down with some kind of flu bug.

Pushing herself up, she went to the door and opened it, startled to see Judy Sawyer standing there. Her neighbor smiled, but Wendy could see concern in her eyes. Judy was as broken up about Wendy's situation as she was—well, almost. Clearly Judy took it as a personal defect that her marshmallow mint sauce had failed.

Judy's pleasant expression faded. "Oh—dear..." she said. "You don't look good."

Wendy smiled wanly, unable to argue the truth. "I think I might be coming down with something. Maybe it would be better if you didn't come in."

"Don't be silly." Taking Wendy's arm, Judy helped her to the couch. "Seth gets everything under the sun, and I never get sick. I tell you what..." Judy sat down beside Wendy and lay the back of her hand against Wendy's forehead. "I've just made some chicken soup. I'll bring over some warm broth."

Wendy's stomach churned, and she swallowed hard. "I—I—thanks, but—"

"At least try to eat," Judy insisted. "You don't feel like you have a temperature. I bet a little broth and some crackers would perk you right up." She patted Wendy's hand. "You've been through a lot these last weeks. I bet you haven't been eating right, that's all."

Wendy shrugged, not knowing what to say. If she told the truth, she supposed she hadn't done much more than pick at her food lately. "I've felt fine—really," she said, staring at her lap. "This came on suddenly, tonight. I had an argument with my father and, I felt sick and dizzy. Probably stress."

"Oh?"

When Judy didn't say more, Wendy lifted her glance to meet her neighbor's pensive expression. Judy squeezed Wendy's knee affectionately. "I'll get you some of that broth. Be right back."

"Thanks." Another bout of dizziness made her woozy. Squeezing her eyes shut, she slumped back.

In a short a time Judy reappeared with a quart jar of golden liquid and a box of crackers. "The broth's still warm. Let me put it in a bowl for you."

Pulling her lips between her teeth, Wendy tried not to gag. But the groan that issued up from her throat couldn't be completely stifled.

Judy came over and sat beside Wendy, laying the jar and cracker box on the coffee table. She touched Wendy's hand. "I know this is none of my business, but do you think you might be—"

"Knock, knock?"

Wendy and her companion looked toward the open door. A tall, slender brunette in a chic black business suit smiled at them. A slim leather briefcase hung from her shoulder. Wendy's heart plummeted a ridiculous distance, considering Josh was no longer her concern. But why did his attorney have to be so gorgeous?

"Miss Hanfield?" she asked hesitantly, clutching at the hope that the beauty in black was selling bibles or makeup, or giving away puppies, and wasn't actually one of Josh's legal eagles.

"Yes, I'm Faith Hanfield." She indicated the apartment with a nod. "May I come in?"

"Oh, you've got company." Judy stood. "I'll go." Glancing back down at Wendy, she said, "Try to eat some broth."

Disconcerted by the beautiful lawyer's presence and the well-meant interference of her neighbor, Wendy was momentarily speechless. "Well—I—"

"Are you ill, Mrs. Raven?" the attorney asked, her expression changing to one of kind concern. "Would you rather I come back another time?"

"She was a little dizzy earlier and her stomach is upset," Judy volunteered, walking to the door. With a friendly touch on the lawyer's arm, Judy said, "Try to get her to eat something."

"It's just a cold, I'm sure," Wendy called after Judy. "Thanks for the broth and crackers."

At the door Judy turned and waved. "I'll check on you before I go to the court house tomorrow." A moment later, Judy was gone, leaving Wendy and the striking lawyer to stare at each other.

After a heartbeat of silence, Faith indicated the couch. "May I?"

Wendy felt like a fool—a dizzy, nauseous fool. "Oh—I'm sorry." She patted the sofa. "Please join me."

Faith moved silently and gracefully across the rug, taking a seat beside Wendy. "You're sure you're feeling all right?"

"Just stress or—lack of sleep or—or something," Wendy mumbled. "I hope I'm not contagious."

The lawyer laughed. "My six-year-old has brought home so many germs from school, I'm sure I'm immune."

Wendy smiled in spite of her mood. The woman had a friendly way about her, even if she was beautiful, and—at the very least—Josh's confidante. Faith's expression grew somber. "We really could postpone this. I know how stressful this sort of thing can be."

Wendy sucked in a fortifying breath, feeling slightly less ill. "No—let's get it done."

"If you say so." All business now, Faith opened her briefcase. She drew out a sheaf of official-looking documents. "Here are the divorce papers. Please read them, then sign where I've indicated."

Wendy took the papers, willing her hands not to shake. Unable to focus on the words that would end her marriage, she flipped listlessly through the pages. "It looks very legal.'' Another wave of nausea hit her and she pressed her lips together.

''That's what I do—make things very legal.''

Wendy scanned the legalese feeling utterly worn down. Discarded.

Faith fished inside her briefcase. ''And here are the papers turning over the company. Once again, I've denoted the places requiring your signature.''

Wendy nodded absently. She scanned the last page of the divorce papers, deciding there was no need to read them. It was best to get it over. ''If you have a pen, I'll...'' Something in what the lawyer just said niggled at her brain and she glanced up. ''What did you say about the company?''

Faith hefted a second sheaf of papers, this one thicker. She handed it to Wendy. ''As I said, the company will be yours as soon as you sign the places I've indicated. You will have complete autonomy to place anyone in charge that you feel—''

''*Mine?*'' Wendy was confused. ''What do you mean, the company will be mine? What company?''

Faith glanced at Wendy, her brow furrowing as though she assumed Wendy had been appraised of this transaction. ''Well—naturally I'm referring to all of Joshua's holdings. Including everything he gained in the merger.'' The attorney studied Wendy, her expression inquiring. ''You didn't know he's giving you Raven-Maxim Enterprises?''

Wendy shook her head, broadsided by this turn of events. ''Has—has he lost his *mind?*''

Faith smiled without humor. ''I've known Mr. Raven for a lot of years, and I've never met a more intelligent, generous employer.'' She shook her head. ''To answer your question, he hasn't lost his mind, Mrs. Raven.'' She held out a golden pen. ''No—his mind is *not* what he's lost.''

Wendy felt as though she'd been struck by lightning. ''But—but does he have the right to give me the company? I mean, since I left him, doesn't the deal fall through?''

Faith pressed the pen into her hand. ''No. Whatever gave you that idea?''

''But—but he tried so hard to make me stay. It couldn't have been—I mean, he didn't really....'' Her sentence died as the impossible began to penetrate. She hardly noticed when Faith took a business card from her briefcase and lifted the golden pen from Wendy's limp fingers, scribbling something on the back of the card.

''Mrs. Raven,'' Faith said quietly, drawing Wendy from her crazy imaginings.

''Hmmm?'' she asked, dazed.

Faith placed the pen into her briefcase. ''Why don't I leave the documents with you? When you've signed them, I'll send one of our paralegals to fetch them.'' She placed her business card on the coffee table, facedown. ''I think I'll send Mark. He's a nice young man, and I have a feeling he might like to meet your neighbor.''

''Judy?'' Wendy asked, startled by the change of subject.

Faith smiled, nodding. ''I have a sense about people. If I send Mark, will you introduce him to Judy?''

Wendy nodded. Judy could certainly use a nice man in her life. ''Of course. It would be my pleasure.''

''That's fine.'' Faith held out a hand and Wendy accepted it. ''Goodbye, Mrs. Raven. Take care of yourself.''

After a few seconds or a thousand light-years, Wendy couldn't be sure, she realized her apartment door was closed and the lawyer was gone. Disoriented, her senses spinning, she leaned forward, pressing the flat of her hands against her temples. She was so dizzy, so confused. Josh was giving her a divorce—but he was also giving her *everything* he'd worked for all his life? That didn't make any sense—unless he really did—unless he meant everything he'd....

Her glance caught on Faith's business card. Something scrawled there caught her eye. ''Dr. John Morris, Obstetrics.'' Underneath, the lawyer had penned, ''I have a sense about people, Mrs. Raven. Make an appointment.''

Wendy read the word aloud. ''Obstetrics.'' She stared at it. But wasn't that the type of doctor who cared for women who were pregnant?

Pregnant!

The truth slammed into her brain, and she stopped breathing.

CHAPTER TWELVE

JOSH shrugged out of his shirt and tossed it on the pile of firewood he'd already chopped. He didn't need the blasted wood. He'd already chopped enough to last him through two years of continuous blizzards. But he had to do something to work off his restless energy.

He'd spent only a few days in Chicago after the disastrous honeymoon, just long enough to draft the documents turning over the company to Wendy. He hadn't been able to concentrate on anything, and even in the crowded city, he'd felt terribly alone. He preferred the seclusion of Raven's Roost, and had returned nearly two weeks ago. At least, here, he had his memories of the wedding night he'd shared with Wendy.

Wrenching his ax blade out of the stump, he grabbed another section of log and stood it on the tree trunk. With a mighty chop, he split it in two, then tossed the pieces on the growing mountain of firewood. Shifting to get another log, he stopped, listening. A motorboat? He glanced at his watch. A little late in the day for the mail, but he didn't care. He had no interest in what the post might bring. If the truth be told, he had little interest in anything these days.

Drawing in a long breath, he went back to work. Physical exhaustion was his only consolation of late. During this past month, since Wendy ran away, he'd learned how little gratification the acquisition of money and power had ever given him. How many times had he laughed at the old saying "Money can't buy happiness," thinking it sentimental and silly?

These days, alone here in his woodland hideaway, he'd learned how right that adage was. He couldn't conjure up a shred of desire to be the wealthiest man in America anymore. For the first time in his life, Josh felt rudderless, lost, caring for nothing, wanting nothing—but Wendy.

He marked time by driving himself to his physical limits. He might not get much satisfaction out of the sweat of his brow, but at least he got so worn out he could finally fall asleep. It was probably his due that Wendy haunted him even then. He had an ironic thought, wondering if this mountain home was doomed to forever house heartbroken men.

Taking a powerful swing of his ax, he halved another cedar log, taking his frustrations out on hapless wood. Movement out of the corner of his eye caught his attention. Wiping his brow, he turned toward the lake.

Someone was coming up the granite walkway. He straightened, his ax thudding to the ground. Could it be? He sucked in a sharp breath, staring at the figure slowly ascending the distant path.

He began to move toward her. It could be Faith Hanfield with the divorce papers. He hadn't signed them. Couldn't. Not until he actually saw Wendy's signature there. But surely Faith would have mailed them.

He rounded the side of the house. By the time he reached the top of the walk, she was halfway up.

Wendy! His nerves grew taut, his heart rate quickening like an engine running at full throttle.

He hadn't dared hope, but there she was. Walking toward him.

He could barely control himself. *Hold on there,*

brother, he counseled inwardly. *She might be here with an altogether reasonable, unromantic question about the business. Don't go grabbing her and kissing her again like a blasted fool!*

Forcing a calm facade, he waved. ''Hi, stranger.'' He grimaced. *Don't remind her that she ran away, idiot!*

She waved back. She carried no suitcase, and she held only a thick manila envelope. Disconcerted, he scanned the dock. No suitcase. But the boat was gone. What did this mean? Maybe the motorboat was supposed to return for her—soon. And the envelope she carried? *Hell.* Had she brought the divorce papers, herself? Why? Revenge? He kept the smile on his face, though he wanted to throw something—his fist through a wall, to be exact.

''It's good to see you,'' he said honestly. She was only a few steps away now. With great unwillingness, he stuffed his hands into his jeans' pockets.

''It's good to see you, too, Josh.'' She came to a stop on the slab where he stood—only an arm's length away. She smiled, but it was indefinite, not the full, sweet I-love-you smile he longed for.

She wore a pink sundress. She looked so beautiful. He'd never realized she had a cruel streak. This was torture. Hell on earth. He could detect her scent and inhaled guiltily. Blast! It would be better to get this over before he did something stupid. ''Is that for me?'' He nodded toward the envelope.

''Yes.'' She didn't hand it to him, just looked at his face, her expression serious. ''Could we—go inside?''

He felt like a jerk—not a particularly unique experience lately. ''Sure.'' Against stern orders, his hand slid from his pocket and took her elbow. He cursed himself, but once he touched her, he couldn't let her go.

She didn't pull away, but she was probably merely

being polite. He cleared his throat, opening the door for her to precede him. "Al will be glad to see you," he offered, deciding inane conversation was better than strained silence.

Wendy's expression eased, and almost became a smile, but not quite. "I've missed her. How is she?"

Flapping wings heralded a new presence in the entryway. Talons dug into Josh's bare shoulder. "*Caw-caw!* I love *Josh!* I *love* Josh!"

He winced from the embarrassing reminder of their disastrous past. "I'm sorry about that," he murmured. "She doesn't unlearn things very easily."

It startled him when Wendy took his fingers and led him into the living room. "Let's sit down, Josh."

He frowned at her serious manner. Apparently she wasn't happy to be reminded of their marriage—or the soft feeling she'd once had for him. When they were seated on the couch, he extended a hand. "I presume you want me to sign those?"

She handed him the packet. "Yes, if you don't mind."

He gave the envelope a black look. With a heaviness in his belly, he dumped the contents on the pine coffee table. A pen clattered out with the papers. He forced back a curse. "You thought of everything, I see."

"I hope so."

He lifted the sheaf of papers and scanned the cover page. "These aren't the divorce papers," he said, confused. "These are for company ownership." He looked at her. "I don't understand."

She picked up the pen and held it toward him. "I've had them drawn up, making you the CEO. You see, I've decided to retire from big business. I'd rather stay home and decorate the nursery—if it's all right with you. Of course we'll have to find a house, first—with lots of rooms for the children.''

He listened, baffled, opened his mouth to speak, then stared again. ''What?''

She smiled, a real I-love-you smile, and it filled him with a warmth unlike anything he'd ever experienced. Taking his face in her hands, she whispered, ''If I'm going to have the baby, darling. You really should do something.'' She kissed him lightly. ''Don't you think?''

Intense pleasure coursed through him, making him go hot and cold and definitely delirious. Had she said what he thought she'd said? ''You're pregnant?'' he asked, his voice hushed.

She nodded. ''Happy?''

''Happy?'' he echoed, as the storm clouds that shrouded his heart disappeared. ''Happy?'' He stood up, sweeping her into his arms. Al squawked and flapped to safety.

Wendy giggled and grasped his neck. ''Yes. Are you?''

''Are you?'' he whispered, still unable to believe his good fortune.

She nodded, kissing his jaw. ''I think it's illegal to be this happy, Josh.'' Lovely tears shimmered on her lashes.

Lord! He'd missed those big, purple eyes! ''If it's illegal, then we're both going to jail, my love.'' He carried her toward the staircase, vowing, ''I love you.''

She snuggled against him. ''I know.'' He felt her brush a kiss against his throat. ''By the way, I fired Daddy.''

Josh stopped and stared. ''You didn't.''

She shrugged sheepishly. ''Well, I gave him a nice

golden parachute. I didn't think you'd mind. I'm sure someday he'll learn to love golf.''

Josh couldn't hold back a rumble of laughter. He carried her halfway up the stairs before he halted, suddenly worried. ''Say, can you—I mean, are you feeling—er—can we...?''

She touched his cheek, love sparkling in her eyes. ''Yes, we can. And if I have anything to say about it, we will for days and days. Why do you think I didn't bring any clothes?''

''Josh loves Wendy,'' Al whispered from a nearby perch on the banister.

Wendy glanced at the bird, then smiled up at her husband. ''I like that, darling.''

He kissed the tip of her nose. ''Before today is over,'' Josh promised softly, ''that's not all you're going to like.''

Eight months later, Josh was reminded of the vital lesson his marriage to Wendy had taught him—about the great and abiding power of love. Neither the lure of wealth nor prominence could begin to rival the glimmering beauty of his wife's eyes as she presented him with their newborn son.

MILLS & BOON®

Next Month's Romance Titles

Each month you can choose from a wide variety of romance novels from Mills & Boon®. Below are the new titles to look out for next month from the Presents™ and Enchanted™ series.

Presents™

THE MARRIAGE DECIDER	Emma Darcy
TO BE A BRIDEGROOM	Carole Mortimer
HOT SURRENDER	Charlotte Lamb
THE BABY SECRET	Helen Brooks
A HUSBAND'S VENDETTA	Sara Wood
BABY DOWN UNDER	Ann Charlton
A RECKLESS SEDUCTION	Jayne Bauling
OCCUPATION: MILLIONAIRE	Alexandra Sellers

Enchanted™

A WEDDING WORTH WAITING FOR	Jessica Steele
CAROLINE'S CHILD	Debbie Macomber
SLEEPLESS NIGHTS	Anne Weale
ONE BRIDE DELIVERED	Jeanne Allan
A FUNNY THING HAPPENED...	Caroline Anderson
HAND-PICKED HUSBAND	Heather MacAllister
A MOST DETERMINED BACHELOR	Miriam Macgregor
INTRODUCING DADDY	Alaina Hawthorne

On sale from 5th March 1999

H1 9902

Available at most branches of WH Smith, Tesco, Asda, Martins, Borders, Easons, Volume One/James Thin and most good paperback bookshops

disabilities - 0114 2718806
handsworth.